'If poetry was the supreme literary form of the First World War then, as if in riposte, in the Second World War, the English novel came of age. This wonderful series is an exemplary reminder of that fact. Great novels were written about the Second World War and we should not forget them.'

WILLIAM BOYD

'It's wonderful to see these four books given a new lease of life because all of them are classic novels from the Second World War written by those who were there, experienced the fear, anguish, pain and excitement first-hand and whose writings really do shine an incredibly vivid light onto what it was like to live and fight through that terrible conflict.'

JAMES HOLLAND, Historian, author and TV presenter

'The Imperial War Museum has performed a valuable public service by reissuing these four absolutely superb novels covering four very different aspects of the Second World War. I defy you to choose which is best: I keep changing my mind!'

ANDREW ROBERTS, author of *Churchill: Walking with Destiny*

PRAI

'A tremendous rediscovery of a brilliant novel. Extremely well-written, its effects are both sophisticated and visceral. Remarkable.'

WILLIAM BOYD

'David Piper's moving, wholly convincing, and deeply personal account of the muddle and terror of the 1941-42 Malayan campaign will stay with the reader for a very long time. The denouement is one of the most powerful in all Second World War fiction.'

ANDREW ROBERTS, author of *Churchill: Walking with Destiny*

TRIAL BY BATTLE

David Piper

First published in Great Britain as
Trial by Battle by Peter Towry,

First published in this format in 2019 by
IWM, Lambeth Road, London SE1 6HZ
iwm.org.uk

ISBN 978-1-912423-08-8

A catalogue record for this book is available from the British Library.

Printed and bound by CPI Group (UK) Ltd, Croydon CR0 4YY

Cover illustration by Bill Bragg
Design and art direction by Clare Skeats

About the Author

David Piper (1918–1990)

Perhaps best known as an art historian and museum director, DAVID PIPER studied Modern and Medieval Languages at Cambridge from 1937 to 1940. During the Second World War he served with the Indian Army, training as an officer in Bangalore before joining the 4th Battalion, 9th Jat Regiment. The battalion arrived in Malaya in January 1942, and Piper's first novel, *Trial by Battle*, vividly describes the confused jungle fighting in that campaign which led to his capture near Singapore. From February 1942 to September 1945 Piper was a Japanese prisoner of war, first in Singapore and later Taiwan.

After the war Piper married and returned to Britain, beginning a career in art history at the National Portrait Gallery in London. He spent twenty years there (the last three as Director), before becoming the Director of the Fitzwilliam Museum in Cambridge in 1967. In 1973 he became the first Director of the Ashmolean Museum in Oxford.

David Piper published a number of books on art history alongside five novels under the pseudonym Peter Towry (Towry being his middle name). *Trial by Battle* was the first of these novels, focusing on his experience of the Second World War. He was knighted in 1983.

Introduction

War literature is often associated with the First World War, with an explosion of the genre in the late 1920s. Erich Maria Remarque's *All Quiet on the Western Front* was a bestseller and later made into a Hollywood film, while generations of schoolchildren have grown up on a diet of the poetry of Wilfred Owen and the words of Siegfried Sassoon.

Yet the novels of the Second World War – or certainly those written by individuals who had first-hand experience of that war – are often forgotten. First published in 1959 under the pseudonym Peter Towry, *Trial by Battle* very much deserves to be remembered, and to be part of the literary canon as a 'wartime classic'. Its author David Piper was an officer educated at Cambridge who went on to become a distinguished art historian and the director of several national museums. The novel tells the story of Alan Mart, from his training in India to the intensive jungle fighting in the Malayan campaign. The critic Frank Kermode described it as 'probably the best English novel to come out of the Second World War', while V.S. Naipaul found the writing superb, and the novel to be 'one of the most absorbing and painful books about jungle warfare that I have read'. The jungle was an alien environment for all the British, Indian and Australian soldiers fighting in Malaya. Very few novelists of the Second World War come close to Piper in evoking the claustrophobia, heat and intensity of this theatre. This very welcome reprint will bring this forgotten war novel to a new readership.

***

At the opening of the novel, the protagonist Alan Mart has just arrived in India, where Sam Holl is put in charge of Mart to show him 'how an infantry battalion in the Indian Army should be run'. On the outbreak of the Second World War India was still the 'jewel in the crown' of the British Empire. The Indian Army was a part of the army based in India (alongside the British Army); this army was the main instrument of control for both internal security and defence of the borders, particularly the North West Frontier. Up until the Second World War, the Indian Army was largely run by British officers in charge of Indian troops.

The huge expansion of the Indian Army at the beginning of the war meant that there was a desperate need for trained officers – hence Mart's posting to this unfamiliar location. In 1939 there were just under 200,000 soldiers in the Indian Army, with only 1,912 British officers and 344 Indian officers. (In contrast, by the end of the war there were over two million in the army with c. 36,438 British officers and 15,747 Indian officers. It had become the largest volunteer army in the world.) In 1940 three officer training schools were set up in India to accommodate the expansion of the officer corps (Alan Mart attends one of these, after leaving university). Following their training, newly commissioned officers elected to join their regiments in the Indian Army. David Piper, for example, attended Bangalore Officer Training School and then joined the 4th Battalion, 9th Jat Regiment. Then, just like Alan Mart, he underwent the signals course at Poona, becoming the signals officer in the battalion. The novel is very much based on his own experience.

The opening line of the novel introduces Mart to Holl, and theirs is the central relationship throughout the book. The contrast between the hard-drinking regular Indian Army officer, Holl, and the inexperienced wartime officer, Mart, is very apparent from the word go. In the first half of the novel, this manifests itself in Alan's rather bizarre decision to turn down a relatively easy and safe posting, teaching German to fellow officers in Simla. After a confrontation with Holl – and perhaps out of a desire to see action himself – Alan rather baffles his adjutant by rejecting the position ('Did you say you did *not* want to go to Simla?'). Mart's actions seem nonsensical, even to him. Later on in the novel, as Alan's experiences leave him desensitised to army life, he develops a grudging, new found respect for Holl, the experienced soldier. He has adapted to cope with the fighting life both through the army, but also under Holl's guidance. In the closing chapters, in the most desperate of situations, it is Holl who Alan seeks:

He tried to find out whether Sundar had any idea what had happened during the night, but Sundar had none, apart from the certainty that there had been a great battle with great noise. For all Alan knew, Holl might still be there; there was no sound of action anywhere near, only the rumble far away to the south. His thought stopped at Holl as a terminus. There he had to go.

If we see Alan's shock at Holl's behaviour earlier in the novel, what the reader also witnesses is the intensity of army life, and more specifically the culture shock of being in a different country, so far from the familiar. This is revealed on numerous occasions, particularly Mart's rather uncomfortable relationship with the men he commands. He struggles with his relationship with his orderly Sundar Singh – 'Orderly? You mean he's a soldier? But he's a child. Can't be a day more than fourteen' – and finds effective communication with the men he commands extremely difficult:

He tried to talk to them and they answered 'Yes, sahib,' or 'No sahib,' in the gaps of his stumbling Urdu. They seem unknowable: they seemed to wish to know, at least to understand what he wished, as much as he did; there were foggy smiles, gestures left incomplete in the air, but there was no contact. He got to feel very little more at home with them yet; he certainly did not feel for one moment in command of them.

All of this combines to build a rather chaotic picture of ill-preparedness, and the alienation experienced by Alan in such unfamiliar surroundings.

Indeed if the officer training is insufficient, the six weeks spent with the training battalion for the Indian soldiers does not bode well for the fighting ahead. In effect the Viceroy Commissioned Officers (a level of officers between non-commissioned officers and the British commissioned officers) are the link between the men and the British officers. Holl tells Mart: 'They'll be very kind to you. Once the Hindu VCOs have drunk you under the table on tumblers of desi whisky and you've overeaten of goat curry with the Mosel ones, they'll love you like a son.' The paternalistic relationship of the British officers and the Indian soldiers is very evident in the book, sometimes bordering on racism, and problems with communication abound.

Evocative as these opening chapters of the novel are – where we see Mart's youth and inexperience, his uneasy relationship with Holl, the confused and chaotic nature of some of the preparations – the book's supreme strength lies in its depictions of jungle warfare once the men arrive in Malaya. The evocation of the claustrophobia, the heat, the fear and the tension can only be drawn from direct experience. Notable is Alan's realisation early on that his equipment simply will not work in the jungle – a terrain almost depicted as an enemy itself:

> *'Drums, sir' said Alan fiercely, 'We might be able to work something out with native drums.'*
>
> *The glaring eyes popped, and blinked rapidly. Then they glazed with a wary caution. Alan saw Scrapings' gaze wander and tangle in angry lost bewilderment amongst the endless trees, and recognising the feeling, his own anger vanished as he suddenly he felt the full weight of responsibility on those elderly thin shoulders.*
>
> *'We'll think of something, sir,' he said gently but confidently.*
>
> *Later that day, a message reached him from the C.O. He was to proceed at once into Malacca again, and corner all native drums that might be available.*

Scenes of this nature are an accurate reflection of the reality of Piper's true experience, as noted in the regimental history. From December 1941 to May 1942 the British Empire suffered the most humiliating series of defeats in its history, as Hong Kong, Malaya, Borneo, Singapore and Burma fell in rapid succession to the Imperial Japanese Army. The Fall of Singapore in February 1942 was considered by the British Prime Minister, Winston Churchill, 'the worst and largest capitulation in history'. The Japanese had overrun the numerically superior Commonwealth forces in Malaya in just over two months, resulting in more than 130,000 troops entering captivity. As a lieutenant comments in *Trial by Battle*: 'Never have so many run so fast and so far from so few'. As with the 'native' drums scene, on numerous occasions we see how the men are not prepared for the theatre into which they have been sent – 'I'm afraid our desert training will be somewhat supernumerary', is the dry comment from the Commanding Officer.

Once in the jungle itself, the text becomes fraught with tension and a sense of isolation:

> *He looked up from the map at the solid bare trunks that dwindled away from them but nevertheless closed their sight at a radius of a hundred yards or so. They seemed like prison bars arrayed wilfully as a maze. It seemed to him that one could not hope within reason to hold country like this without much less than a man per tree, and he looked to Holl to say so, but swallowed the remark.*

When Alan first sees action – having earlier heard the swirling rumours that 'the Japanese take no prisoners' – the text vividly describes his scramble for survival when his jeep is hit and he and Holl must try to make their way back to their own troops. As the situation becomes more desperate, the light-heartedness that tinges some of the novel's opening chapters dissipates. Alan, and the reader, are far from the heady days of training at Poona. Particularly visceral and moving is the scene in which Mart feels he has no choice but to leave his wounded with the Australian padre, knowing what their fate will be:

> *The throb and racket of the final Japanese attack had begun a mile or so away. Arcs of fire, red, yellow, orange, streamed across the sky; flares splashed glaring whiter and brighter than the moon, and sank slow as thistledown. The display raged in brilliant and beautiful violence, seeming to come from fore and aft of the position they had just abandoned, for perhaps twenty minutes, half an hour – then, over the deep clamour of explosives, there came the howl, thinned by distance but*

piercing eardrums like a glacier wind, of the Japanese infantry going in for the kill.

Alan's eyes closed, and he rocked where he stood. The triumphant maddened howl was edged now by a scream that reached into the bowels of the little group who stood there listening, dragging every nerve in their bodies out searing through the skin. When Alan's eyes opened again, the tears were flowing down his face, blurring the southern sky that now was lit by the pulsing leaping flame from trucks on fire.

***

David Piper served with the 4th/9th Jats in the Malayan campaign. They arrived in theatre in early January 1942, and fought alongside the Australians at Muar. Piper was the signals platoon commander in the battalion. He along with Major White (second-in-command) went missing on 18 January when their car was ambushed on the way to brigade headquarters and their driver killed. They spent the night by the side of the road and attempted to return to the battalion the following day. Faced by Japanese tanks, they returned through the jungle – exactly as Alan Mart does in the novel. On 19 January 1942, the battalion was ordered to join up with the Australians. However they were heavily attacked, and in the confusion there were many casualties. Piper, having got lost, managed to make his way back to the 2/29th Australian Battalion but later became a prisoner of war. Mart's experience in *Trial by Battle* is thus almost an exact replica of Piper's own time in the jungle.

After the surrender at Singapore David Piper was a prisoner of war in Changi and then Taiwan (years later he wrote a very moving memoir and diary of his time in Shirakawa camp in Taiwan, *I Am Well, Who are You?*). In 1944, in what was considered a major turning point for the war in South East Asia, the Japanese Army suffered defeat at the hands of the British and Commonwealth 14th Army at the Battles of Kohima and Imphal, and the later battles for Burma (modern day Myanmar). The transformation in the fortunes of the Commonwealth troops, in particular the Indian Army, was in a large part due to the development of jungle warfare doctrine and the resulting improvements in training, tactics and equipment. Unfortunately for many men such as Piper, these developments had come too late.

After the war, Piper returned to Britain and married (he had his own 'Lettice' in real life). He published a number of books on art history and five novels under the pseudonym Peter Towry – *Trial by Battle* was the first, published in 1959. One of the possible reasons for the pseudonym was that some of the men in his battalion were still alive (Towry was his middle name and he had been known as Pete by his old friends). In the foreword to *I Am Well, Who Are You?*, a fellow prisoner of war wrote of Piper: 'I was amused by the ironic detachment with which he coped with the circumstances of being a POW and the extreme modesty with which he regarded his achievements in the post war world. Those of us who had the opportunity to make something of our lives after the war were lucky. Many were not.'

Alan Jeffreys
2019

ONE

'AND THIS,' said the adjutant, 'is Lieutenant Acting-Captain Holl, known as Sam. Sam, this is Alan Mart, just arrived, first posting from the Cadet College. I'll be detailing him off to you to learn how an infantry battalion in the Indian Army should be run.'

Holl rose from his chair. He seemed to go on rising for an interminable time, lurching from one side to the other, before he found his stature. He was a large-boned man, corded with muscle unsoftened by any spare flesh; his khaki bush-shirt and slacks looked flimsy on him, and his rather small squarish head inadequate as a terminal for the torso. He had pale grey eyes, a thin pale mouth and a thin pale feathering of hair, delicate and shallow as seedlings. His teeth were yellowish, with an exclamation of pure gold on the left-hand side, and he sucked a great deal at them. He was looking cautiously down at Alan, seeming to reserve malevolence rather than judgment.

Alan held out his hand. It was taken in a dry and solid grip.

'What'll you have?' said Holl. He tended to flatten his a's.

Alan saw that Holl seemed to be drinking a small lemonade.

'I'm on the wagon,' said Holl. 'I been naughty. Don't let it fuss you.'

Alan had a beer, and nervously started to ask questions about the unit, which was now his unit. Holl ignored the questions, staring all over Alan in dispassionate stocktaking, and sucking at his teeth.

'You're a bit frail, lad,' he said at last. He put his fingers round Alan's upper arm. 'Christ, what a twig! Come from a good home, three months in the ranks and never a word fired in anger, into a cadet college, and here you are an officer and a gentleman. Well, I wish you luck, son, I wish you luck.' He laid a finger on the side of his nose, waggled his small head, and suddenly turned and left the bar.

'It's all right,' said the adjutant, soothing. 'He's a lamb really; heart of gold as true as his tooth. And the best soldier in the brigade. Drinks too much, that's all; the C.O. had to lay him off alcohol during the week. There was an incident at a tennis party a couple of Sundays ago.'

'Incident?'

'Our Sam,' said the adjutant, 'was stinking. The C.O.'s aunt would tell him about the trouble she was having with one of her sweepers, and Sam in the end told her straight out she was a flat-chested Tory.'

Alan said he didn't know you could say that to your C.O.'s aunt.

'You can't. But Sam said, and he stuck to it, that the words he had really used were: What a fascinating story. And as the aunt is deafish and I perjured myself in favour of Sam's version, all the C.O. did was to blow Sam up to the ceiling, and put him on the water wagon.'

'Oh. You still have tennis parties.'

It was October, 1941, and even in India the war had been on officially for over two years.

'Yes. The women like it. And you may well ask, do we still have women and the answer still is, yes, the women like it.' The adjutant smoothed his moustache cleverly; it was an elusive, rather wispy, job; he looked barely twenty though he was in fact twenty-five, with some years of planting in Assam to his credit. 'But it only happens on Sunday afternoons. Otherwise, you'll find, we work solid. By the way, you've got visiting cards, of course?'

'Of course.' Second-Lieutenant Mart, they said; he had had them engraved in Bombay during his leave. 'I think I'd better go back to my room now and see if my kit's turned up.'

Alan's room was a small wooden box that contained a bed with a wire framework on which was furled, like a canopy, his mosquito net; there was a wooden chair, a table, a rudimentary chest of drawers, and a washbowl on a metal tripod stand. Set in the ceiling was a large electric fan.

Not much of his kit had come.

He walked about his room. He switched a switch and a naked light bulb shone palely. He switched it off, and tried the second switch. With a grunt, the fan heaved into action. He lay down and looked at the fan through the mosquito net. After a while he took a crumpled airmail letter from his breast-pocket and started to read it.

Darling [it said],

I've come up early before term started and I wish I hadn't.

Cambridge is unbearable without you though I ought to be used to it by now what with fifteen months already without you. But the trees have turned and are burning and the river so slow you'd think it must stop and the leaves fall one by one very slowly too. Punting last summer term wasn't at all the same without you, and the food's awful. But it's funny what a lot of people there are about because with the war you'd think there wouldn't be. Of course they're all awful and only ghostly pretenders in your gap and they muck up all the places that belonged to us, but some are less awful than others. Oh, George sends you his love; he's in the... [two lines were here covered by the censor's broad black bar]. *Isn't it marvellous? And he says...* [another blank]. *There was a wonderful party in Gibbs' Building last night at least it would have been wonderful if you had been there and Jimmy said...* [deleted by censor]. *But you must be having some fun, darling. I do hope even in stuffy old India, and I know you'll think I'm a mean old bitch gadding while you serve, but oh, my lamb, it's the nights that are not so good when I can't get away from you and you aren't there. ...*

There was a lot more; but he had read it all through several times already, and it read on the whole less well each time. That bit about the nights particularly which was so pleasing and sad at first reading; but when he came to think about it, they had only ever spent three nights together, and those three nights had been extremely confused. Still, he knew what she meant; it was put like that because she was reading English, no doubt. He sighed, and laid the letter on his breast, and began to count his fingers. He had just registered them all present and correct, and was starting to check on his toes, pressing them one by one against the hot inner soles of his boots, when he realised that he was not alone.

A small round Indian boy stood by his bed; he was wearing a

khaki shirt with the tails out over his shorts, and nothing on his feet. His head was shaven of hair except for one thin six-inch strand that drooped limply from the back. His face shone; his protuberant eyes swam moistly; he was of an attractive, even, warm brown, marred by a large red boil approaching its climax on his cheek. He seemed to be about fourteen.

They looked at each other. The boy was nervous, and looked away. He stood all the while stiffly to attention, but quivered constantly.

'Sahib!' he said suddenly, urgently, and Urdu flew out of him.

Alan failed entirely to follow.

The flow diminished, stuttered and stopped; the large eyes swam still with mute popping queries like goldfish.

'What do you want?' said Alan slowly, unravelling his Urdu.

'Sahib.'

'Oh, go away.'

'Sahib.'

'Go away!' Alan was getting cross. '*Jao*! Shoo!'

The boy remained stiffly at attention.

Alan half sat up, fluttering his hands. 'Shoo! shoo!'

From the doorway a roar interrupted him. In the gloom stood Holl.

The boy spun round, and seemed for a moment to be about to prostrate himself. Holl addressed him in fluent Urdu with an oddly cockney accent. Then he turned to Alan. 'This is your orderly. His name's Sundar Singh. What do you want him to do?'

'*Orderly*? You mean he's a soldier? But he's a child. Can't be a day more than fourteen.'

'Oh no. A good seventeen; sixteen anyway. One of the new draft. One hundred and ninety recruits with long service of at least six weeks in the Training Battalion were posted to us last week, to replace one hundred and ninety veterans pinched from us to form the nucleus of the 11th Battalion now forming. I dare say, my boy, you realise we're standing by to proceed overseas on active service; which will be, they do say, in a couple of months at the latest. So far, these one hundred and ninety have just about learned to wear boots. Two months from now, with luck, they'll have learned to squeeze a trigger.'

'Oh.'

'What do you want him to do?'

Alan looked around his bleak room. There didn't seem much an orderly could do in it. Then he thought it would be nice to be tucked up in bed.

'Your kit come yet? No? He'd better go and find it.' Holl spoke to the orderly, who vanished in a flash of eyes and a scurry.

Holl was saying that Alan shouldn't worry about his Urdu. It would come very quickly. 'It has to. There you are, with all those black shining faces turned up to you, waiting for the pearls to drop; you have to say something. I mean you learned the grammar at your Cadet College?'

'Oh yes.' Alan thought of his teacher, his *munshi* at the college. They used to sit for hours under a flame-of-the-forest tree; the *munshi* was a small man, like a spectacled tortoise with halitosis. 'In this poem,' he would say, 'the lights burning in the windows of the bazaar at Bombay remind me of the flowers in my native province which are so jolly.' And his nasal voice would escape like a daddy longlegs into the branches. 'Most beautiful,' he would say. 'Now it is your turn to sing me a song, by your T. S. Eliot perhaps or W. Shakespeare.' He had extraordinarily thick lips that moulded each word separately and a little clumsily. He was a pacifist, and Alan used to mock him about passive resistance until, realising he was being teased, the *munshi* would giggle helplessly. Sometimes, after a particularly gay session, they would sing *Land of Hope and Glory* together, in joint honour of India and of Britain.

'Yes,' said Alan. 'I did the grammar.'

'Time we got over to the Mess,' said Holl. His mood had changed now, to a rather sinister joviality. 'Saturday and gone six-thirty. I'm allowed two whiskies tonight; and two more tomorrow.'

Alan collected himself together; as they left the room, his orderly came up, puffing under a tin trunk and a kit bag.

Holl roared, apparently by an automatic reaction, for no specific purpose. The orderly wobbled, as if attempting a salute, and passed on into Alan's room.

'I thought,' said Alan, 'one wasn't called up till one was eighteen.'

'Oh, they *say* they're eighteen, the blockheads. I've got some I'll swear aren't more than fifteen, if that. It's expected of them by their family. Matter of honour. Poor little sods.'

Holl stopped. He turned and faced Alan.

'But they're the best fighting troops in the world. Except possibly the Gurkhas. But you want to remember that, Mart. The best bloody fighting troops in the world, when trained.'

His prize-fighter head wove from side to side, as if challenging contradiction. Then he turned, and strode on towards the brightly lit windows of the Mess.

Over his shoulder, he added: 'Properly led, of course.'

Fairly early after dinner, but a little tight perhaps, owing to the warm greeting extended to him by his new colleagues, Alan returned to his room. They were not at all like any of his normal friends. There was the second-in-command, a tall loosely built major, stooping and kindly and with an odd impression of walking in step with himself like a yak. There were the company commanders, the senior one, Harold Hockey, rather intimidating, with hauteur, boiled blue eyes and raging moustaches – a professional soldier out of Sandhurst; then a quiet, dour Scotch farmer, built short and square as if of Aberdeen granite, but with mild soft brown eyes and a reserved but very warm smile; there was a round, polished fair man called George Wilkins, like a stockbroker, or what Alan believed stockbrokers to be like, his head as if moulded in a bowler hat, but in fact also a professional Sandhurst soldier. There was Holl, and there was another subaltern well senior to Alan, rather soft and fair, with a rich red mouth that was a little too wet. Alan was not unhappy; they had all been agreeable and friendly in their various ways; only Holl remained somewhat intimidating. He had to report to Holl for horse riding at 5.30 a.m. next morning, and to the adjutant, later in the morning, for elementary initiation into the organisation of the battalion. He was tired now, a little dazed, and he still had to unpack and somehow convert his little wooden room, that smelled of insecticide and old luggage, into a habitable cell before he slept. He had strong nesting habits.

The light was on in his room. His mosquito net was down, and tucked in. Sundar Singh stood by it, looking uncertainly at little piles of clothing, books, equipment and shoes that he had taken out of the still half-full tin trunk, and put on the table.

'You again,' said Alan jovially.

The boy stiffened to attention.

'Better get all this shipshape,' said Alan. 'Shipshape.' The Urdu for shipshape escaped him. He began to laugh.

'Sahib.' His orderly looked at him, suspicious and wounded.

Alan stopped laughing and demonstrated where he wanted his clothes put. They did it together, with some merriment that at last began to infect the orderly.

'O.K.,' said Alan, at length. 'Run along now.' He added in Urdu: 'Thank you.'

Then, as the orderly was going, he realised that he would need calling – at 5a.m. at the latest. (God! 5a.m.)

'Sepoy!' he said briskly. He was surprised and rather shocked to hear the word. Vividly he remembered the first time an officer had annihilated him into anonymity with the word: *Soldier*! do this, do that.

The boy was back.

'Sundar,' said Alan. He explained that his *chota hazri*, tea and biscuit, should be delivered at quarter of five. From where? he wondered. Where did the boy go to now, to sleep, to burrow, out in the labyrinthine Indian night.

'*Ram ram*,' he said, and put his hands together in the Hindu greeting, as his *munshi* had taught him.

The boy was surprised and flustered; then his face melted into rolls of fat smile, his eyes beamed and his teeth shone; he joined his hands too, and inclined gravely over them.

'*Ram ram*, sahib,' and he was gone.

Alan started undressing. He stopped. Someone was undressing alongside him. He discovered that a large looking-glass had been imported into his room since he had first arrived. Standing in his pants, he looked at himself, thin as twigs, Holl had said, stooping a little at the shoulders. This was all right for a scholar, wrong for a soldier; he straightened them. He had a long, dark, narrow head, with dark eyes looking melancholy under thick dark eyebrows that were scrupulously tidy. It was very silent. He intensified the melancholy, and ran a hand over the blue stubble on his chin. He was just twenty-one, and very old.

A large bug flew blind and loud as a bomber through the window and crashed on the light bulb, falling with a thud to the floor.

'God,' thought Alan. 'I shouldn't call that boy by his Christian name. If it was his Christian name. Hindu name. Whatever. Not done.'

He raised a foot to crush the bug that lay on its back, waving feeble legs in the air. Then he did not put his foot on it, but, with infinite distaste and the aid of a sheet of paper, threw it out of the door.

He returned to his face in the glass; it was at any rate still there when he sought it.

'You bloody hypocrite,' he said to the long melancholy face, which thereupon looked smug. He erased the smugness. '*Mon lecteur. Mon frère*. You officer, you. You bloody murderer.'

He climbed in through the mosquito net into bed. He lay on his back, stretched stiffly out. In the dim haze of the net it was like a shrine; the sheet settled on him as a shroud. He began to think of Lettice; here was the night and here was he and here she was not. He thought of her belting down King's Parade on a bicycle, her skirts floating, her fair hair in a flood, a predatory look in her blue eyes. Were her eyes blue? He thought about her eyes with some anguish. Maybe they were grey, but grey like an English summer morning sky unveiling to the sun. But he couldn't remember really; his stomach began to hollow with loss, and love to mourn in him like a dog that has seen its master die. Agitated, he shifted, and cracked his fingers, and began to count them. They were all there.

'For five and five make ten, you see, so I'm alive, and I am me,' he muttered, but not with great conviction.

'You clamber on,' said Holl. 'Once on, ensure that you're facing to the front, that is, with a clear view between the horse's ears, not over its arse; grasp the reins firmly but lightly with the hands, grip equally firmly with the knees, and bash the bastard with your heels. The animal will then proceed.'

Alan objected that he had always understood that horses wore saddles.

'The trouble with the public schules,' said Holl primly, 'is that they don't teach men the facts of life.' With marvellous swiftness he blew into a red rage, and roared: 'Get up and *bash*!'

With the help of a smirking *sais*, Alan got up. The horse's back was unfriendly, and too wide. He seized the reins.

'For God's sake!' said Holl, demonstrating. 'You're not reefing a windjammer! Now. Bash with your heels.'

Cautiously, Alan bashed.

The horse turned its head, and looked at him.

Holl roared, and simultaneously flicked the horse smartly with his stick. In a matter of seconds the horse had passed through all intermediary stages into full gallop, and then was airborne over a small dry gully, where Alan left it.

He lay in a windless void darkness constricted by fire. Presently a harsh braying took on red-rimmed substance, and became Holl, who stood over him, at least ten feet high, pulsating with laughter. Then Holl stooped, and helped him up with a surprisingly gentle dexterity.

'That was really funny. I appreciated that,' said Holl, as the *sais* trotted up with the recaptured horse. 'Now. Up you get. And *grip*! And don't go so fast. Trot, to start with.'

It struck Alan that Holl was mad: a dangerous lunatic. He turned and started to limp in the direction of the camp. A sibilant ejaculation of invective stopped him as if with a leash.

Rather hesitantly, he started to answer back in kind.

'Uh've to remind you,' said Holl in a sad, heavy voice, 'that I'm your superior officer. Climb on that horse and let's have no more argument, there's a good gutless boy. And *bash* it!'

Alan stared at him. Holl's eye leant sternly back on him, considerately but mercilessly stern as Abraham's loving eye on Isaac before sacrifice. Then one pale blue winked like a hen's.

Alan all but hit him. Then he swallowed, turned, and got back on the horse again. Holl nodded gravely, and mounted his own animal.

Alan was still wondering sickly what it was in that eye that had compelled him to remount, when he fell off again.

'Come, come,' said Holl. 'You're not trying.'

Clumsily, Alan climbed back again. Holl looked at him.

'Straighten your back,' he said. Then he sniffed, and sucked, still staring. 'How old are you?'

'Twenty-one.'

'Oh. I thought maybe you were about eighteen.'

'My mother always says I look younger than I really am,' said Alan.

Holl whistled. Then he looked sharply and suspiciously at him.

They moved off.

Four more times that morning Alan fell, while the Indian sun rose higher and hotter over the brown plain, and exhaustion gradually numbed his apprehension of the high horse. All the while Holl pranced and caprioled about him, as though his horse were but a perfectly attuned extension of his own powerful thighs; when he decided at last that it was time for breakfast, he was in high spirits. He beat Alan on the back, exclaiming that there was a vague possibility they'd make a soldier out of him yet. 'I can tell you, when you arrived yesterday, Christ, I thought, they've wished another wet on to us, like Johnson before you. Still drunk with his mother's milk he was; we flogged him to Intelligence inside three weeks.'

Outside the Mess he paused, and bent that kindly considerate eye on Alan again. 'You wouldn't by any chance be a pansy?'

Alan gaped at him. 'No.'

'Well, that's all right then. No offence.' But Holl did not at once go on into the Mess. 'That bit about your mother. You were pulling my leg, weren't you?'

'No.'

Alan went on into the Mess, leaving Holl staring after him. As he washed his hands, and splashed cool water on to his face, his mind cleared a little. Sorely, he thought that perhaps he had scored a point, even if only a very small one. But when he went into breakfast, he found Holl in the middle of a vivid description, with picturesque analogies to sexual attitudes, of Alan's falls from the horse. As

Alan ate his eggs, he conducted a searching scrutiny in his memory for anyone more repulsive than Holl; he found no one. Suddenly he realised that he was being addressed.

'Call me Sam,' said Holl. 'We'll be all right. We'll win this war.'

Later that morning, the adjutant told Alan that Scrapings had thought that Alan would be Signals officer. Scrapings was the name by which the C.O., whom Alan had still to meet, was invariably known. Very likely, the adjutant said, that was how it would be, but tomorrow was Monday, and on Mondays Scrapings was temperamental and had a way of reversing any previous week's decisions that were reversible.

'On Mondays, life is tricky, because Scrapings blows up punctually somewhere between eleven and twelve hundred hours. Then I scrape him off the ceiling, dust him down, and we're all set till next Monday. Hence "Scrapings." He knocks hell out of his liver every Sunday with too much curry. But you needn't worry. The havildar who's looking after the Signals platoon is the best we've got, and anyway you'll be attached mainly to Sam for the first week or two. Must be able to take over a fighting company, you see.'

The adjutant walked Alan round the lines, through bleak long wooden huts and past rows of wooden bed frames, freshly scrubbed and airing in the sun; past rows and groups of Indian soldiers in various degrees of Sunday undress but stiffening to attention on their long, thin, dark legs as the officers passed. He introduced Alan to the Viceroy Commissioned Officers, the platoon commanders, sturdy men with easy smiles, and years of soldiering also easy and confident in their bearing. They abashed Alan as no British N.C.O. had ever done.

'It's all right,' said the adjutant. 'They'll be very kind to you. Once the Hindu V.C.O.s have drunk you under the table on tumblers of desi whisky and you've overeaten of goat curry with the Moslem ones, they'll love you like a son. They'll be very kind.'

'Why?'

'What?'

'They bloody well oughtn't to be,' Alan almost said but instead he said, he meant: good. It was a relief when they returned to the squarish hut that served as the Officers' Mess; the Indian lines affected him almost like claustrophobia.

The battalion paraded daily for work, as Alan found with a shock, at 5a.m., or soon after, and the officers worked pretty solidly through the day until about 7p.m. He had more breaks than his colleagues, at least until a certain amount of miscellaneous office work began to be unloaded on to him, but even so was too tired to do anything at the end of the day except go to bed. Mostly he watched, which is tiring. He watched Sam Holl supervising the training of the new drafts, and was astonished and touched by the urgent, almost tender, anxiety with which Holl, and all the other officers, brooded over the training of their troops. His relations with his own Signal platoon were distant and ambivalent; in theory he was in command, in practice he was not to take over until his return from the Signals Course at Poona, which he was to attend as soon as a vacancy showed for him.

Meanwhile he agreed with what he hoped was a judicious air of wisdom to the programmes drawn up by the Signals havildar, and watched the signallers buzzing Morse nimbly to and fro, not understanding a dot of it. Sometimes he would attend the C.O., a thin man of a remarkably elderly forty-five with aggressive iron-grey moustaches and a wild, rather romantic, expression, as he walked about the battalion's business. He watched the brown faces of the troops, puzzled like children when they did not understand, splitting open with mirth when they were amused, or greyed over with dust, bumping along like flotsam on the slow current of a route march, vacant and alien. He saw them stand high and meagre as storks, anchored on the ground by the sledge-hammer boots on their too thin legs; he saw them squat with their hands trailing in the dust over their knees in front, their khaki shirts out over their shorts behind. He heard their guttural talk, heard their hawk and saw them spit betel red; he smelled them, rancid seeming as the *ghi* in which they cooked. He tried to talk to them and they answered 'Yes, sahib,' or 'No, sahib,' in the gaps of his stumbling Urdu. They seemed unknowable; they seemed to wish to know, at least to understand what he wished, as much as he did; there were warm foggy smiles, gestures left incomplete in the air, but there was no contact. He got to feel very little more at home with them yet; he certainly did not feel for one moment in command of them.

The whole battalion was out, straggling across the dusty plain. There was to be an exercise involving aircraft. Alan marched with Holl, who seemed very cross. Upon Alan commenting on this, Holl said that Alan ought to be cross too when he saw what happened.

Presently there was noise like a small distant motor-bicycle. Then Alan saw a tiny two-seater Moth aeroplane cavorting along from the west as if on a rather bumpy road; it passed overhead, looking as though it must fall down at any moment. Two leather-helmeted heads were clearly visible in the cockpits.

On the ground, orders were shouted and arms made wide imperious gestures. After some confusion, during which many soldiers stood stock still, staring up, and some actually waved, brown hands friendlily fluttering, teeth shining, the battalion dispersed and went half-heartedly to ground. The Moth bumbled back, and the man in the rear cockpit began to drop white objects, one by one, over the side, leaning out carefully.

'What on earth?' said Alan.

'Paper bags filled with flour,' said Holl, snarling. He swore fiercely at two sepoys who were kneeling up to see the aeroplane properly. The plane worked its way to and fro several times until presumably it had no bags left.

Alan had started to laugh, helplessly; all the officers seemed so cross, but fifty yards away, one of the sepoys had sustained a near miss, and was showing off his whitened shirt, proudly smiling like a woman in an advertisement for washing powder.

Alan was interrupted by Holl, who tolled like bells: 'What d'you think these poor oafs are going to do in the desert when the tanks of which they've never seen one – when the planes of which most of 'em have just seen their first – come at them? Christ, it makes me weep!'

Alan thought Holl was being pompous; he asked if there weren't any other planes, more modern, in India.

Still in the same tolling voice, Holl said: 'There is rumoured to be one. In a museum, near Karachi.'

Above them, the machine made a final run, so low that they seemed almost to be able to touch it from the ground. The man in the rear cockpit was grinning white under his goggles, and waving gaily. Holl heaved up from his prostrate position, and was crouching as if for the start of a spring. Then he slowly straightened, and his right arm came up and over, heavy as a windmill sail, in the order for his company to advance.

The next day would be Sunday again. At dinner, the adjutant announced that, not having been to bed before two all week, he personally was going to have a nice lie-in. Alan said that would suit him too.

'Second-Lieutenant Mart,' said Holl, 'will report to me for horse exercise at six hundred hours sharp.'

'Oh, for God's sake!' Alan said. 'This isn't a cavalry regiment.'

'You heard,' said Holl. Alan thought he said it with malice.

Later that evening, emboldened by whisky, he sought out Holl alone.

'Look,' he said, 'why pick on me? I don't *like* horses.'

'I know, chum. That's why. But you will like 'em, by the time I've done with you.'

Alan looked at him, bristling.

'Trouble with you,' said Holl, 'you're wet. Soft. Scared.' He was lying back in a long wicker chair on the veranda of the Mess; he raised a smugly pacifying hand in the darkness, and Alan saw his teeth glint. 'That's all right. That's all right. Eighty per cent of the battalion are the same. It's the natural civilised condition. Or at any rate it's what we've all been educated into, and very dainty too, in peacetime. All I'm going to do is to de-educate you.'

'Therefore teach the whole army to ride gee-gees. You're exactly like the old gentleman who interviewed me when I applied for a commission in the tanks in 1939; history had stopped at 1914, let alone 1919.'

Holl was interested. 'What did they say?'

'They said, very first question: Do you hunt? When I said, No, they said: Lack of opportunity or lack of inclination? That was the one vital qualification for tank officers in World War II.'

'A bit old-fashioned,' said Holl. 'But the principle was sound. And they turned you down, of course?'

'Yes.'

'Quite right too. Only then they had to shove you in the infantry as though it were the dustbin.' A low seething crackle came from the wicker chair, as though Holl were in conflict with it. 'But would you imagine the bastards had the nerve to turn *me* down too? Even though I hunted regularly two days a week, and often more. *But* my father was a small-town baker, and I was expelled from school; so they turned me down. That's what comes of giving your children airs. My poor Dad was very set on us having the advantages, as he called them, that had been denied him, so he half-ruined himself sending us to a public school. Only as he couldn't afford a good public school he sent us to a bad one...'

Holl's voice was getting flatter and flatter. 'Bloody boring it was; right tedious. So I seduced the housemaster's daughter, and they sacked me.'

'My, my. And you eloped to Gretna Green and lived happily ever after.'

'That's enough of that,' said Holl. 'It wasn't so funny. Though I don't know, bits of it were, I suppose, looking back. Flipping little stuck-up snob she was, though tasty. She was crazy about horses like schoolgirls are, and she found out, I mean I told her, that I hunted with one of the snobbiest hunts in England; she wasn't to know I did it, see, by helping in the kennels for nothing and by teaching in a riding school to get my horses free. So I led her up the garden path with tales of the aristocracy and our place in the country, and she followed all the way into the bedroom or rather the hayloft. But when they found out, and I wanted her to go off with me, by then she'd found out my father was a baker. So she threw me out, and the school threw me out, and my Dad threw me out. I worked in a garage for a bit, and then I won some fights and got a job as boxing instructor in an athletics training college...'

His voice seemed set to meander on through his whole life story. Impatiently Alan interrupted to say that that was all very well, but no reason why Holl should take it out on him.

'That was when I took to drink,' said Holl, unheeding. 'Been on it ever since, on and off, since I was seventeen. Seventeen's too young to start, really; ruins a man's wind. Slut,' he added, and was silent for a moment.

Then he said: 'I've never forgiven that bitch. I was in love with her.' A flat and final sadness in this statement, like stones falling into wet mud, suddenly convinced Alan that Holl was near the truth, but even more that he was drunk. He rose to go.

A large hand reached out with remarkable swiftness to restrain him.

'I hadn't finished,' said Holl.

He breathed heavily in the dark for some time, his hand still resting round Alan's like a fetter. Then: 'Bloody snobs!' he whispered.

'You want to keep off the booze,' said Holl. 'A youngster like you. Look at me. I'd have my own battalion by now if it wasn't for the Demon. Simply because, mark you, I happen to be a good soldier, that's why I'd have a command. I've been winning this war since autumn, 1938; just me and old Churchill in there together winning this war. No one else even *knew* about it. But I saw 'em. That time I was over in Frankfurt-on-Main bashing the guts out of those German cruiser-weights who thought they could fight, I saw 'em: regiments, divisions, whole damn' armies of 'em rolling along the autobahns in autumn, '38, and those tanks weren't cardboard either...

'Mark you,' said Holl, and a forefinger prodded the dark, 'I'm not moaning about our fellow-officers, our esteemed colleagues. They're a good lot, as good as you'll find. They *mind*. It's just they don't know about there being a war on; none of 'em seen the Jerry bombers come drooling in at dusk over Kent, like you and me have. And they don't know about *winning*. And I can tell you Jimmie boy...'

Alan said his name wasn't Jimmie.

'Heh?' said Holl. He thought a bit. 'Nor it is. I thought for the moment you were my baby brother.' His baffled thought was almost as palpable in the dark as a trapped bat. 'But you're not,' he said at last, apparently relieved. 'But I was saying about this winning. I can tell you, Mart, it's not just yourself you got to persuade is winning; you've got to make eight hundred cross-eyed yokels, the whole damn' battalion, know they're winning. That's what we've got to do; strip the village fat and cow dung of centuries off these brown boys, till they remember the war and the fighting inside of them, and remember that they're the men who went through the whole of India like a dose of salts whenever it was. If they'll give us another four or five months here and a couple more in the desert to limber up, as, mark you, they promise...' He laughed like a supercharged Bentley starting up. 'They promise. But maybe if we have time, if they'll lay off puking paper bags of flour over us from flying banana boxes, and give us some tommy guns, and carriers, and artillery, and antitank stuff, and wireless, then maybe we *will* have time. But it's going to be close.

'The weeping grief of it is,' said Holl, 'given only time, I could make this unit of poxy sweepers into a masterpiece. And the weeping grief of it is, if they don't give us time, you and me are going to personally conduct a battalion of innocent brown souls into massacre. And that's a sin I'm not prepared to die with, not on my lily-white soul.'

'You're tight,' Alan said, trying to disengage the clutch on his wrist.

'Maybe,' said Holl, with some pompousness. 'Or maybe not. But the fact remains even if sheathed in the lily-white fat of your own soul. You're in this too, officer. You and me, we lead these men in battle. In sim'lar circ'mst'nces it is obligatory to know whether you're coming or going. I suggest that you have no idea whether you're coming or going. Now, that's not right, is it, Mart? Christ, boy, you move like a glutted cow when her bags are full to bursting and the milkmaid's busy with a lover. You moon, boy, like a sex-starved calf. I can't think why I waste time with you; but by God, by the time I've finished with you you'll know yourself so well you'll have to murder the whole world in case they find out too. Which is the object of the exercise. See?'

His grip relaxed on Alan's wrist, and nimbly Alan dodged sideways out of his chair before it could trap him again.

'Good night,' he said, with some hauteur.

Holl did not answer; he had slumped, vastly derelict, in the long wicker chair.

Alan walked back to his room, a little dizzy. Never had he been hit so hard and so often by so many platitudes. He thought that Holl, even if drunk, must be going mad. And where had he got the liquor from?

He saw that the light was on in his room. He stopped, looking in through the window. Sundar Singh was tucking his mosquito net in round his bed; the long strand of hair on his shaven head flipped to and fro as he moved. Alan had by now found out at least one account of the purpose of this strand of hair; it served as a handle, according to tradition, by which God lifted one to Heaven when one died. If so, Alan thought, the boy should either grow the strand thicker, or go slimming, for if lifted by it in his present stoutness, he would certainly break it with his weight. He was moving about the room now, gently, softly, and somehow blindly like a moth, bumping in a cushioned way. He was not doing anything, just touching. His fingers caressed Alan's books, and traced the outline of an ashtray; then one finger rested tentatively on a key of the open portable typewriter. The type arm stood up, jerkily. Gently, Sundar moved it up and down, his head on one side; then, as he took his finger off, the arm fell back with a sharp click, and the boy jumped back guiltily from the table. He stood quite still for a moment, apparently listening, until delicately he approached the table again, and, after a couple of feints, picked up Alan's travelling clock in both hands. He peered at it very closely, and then put it to his ear. Rapt, he stayed, with the clock to his ear, and an infinitely foolish, drugged smile slowly swamped his face; his brown eyes almost vanished up under their lids, and the whites gleamed.

Alan's stomach contracted, and he swallowed sickly; there followed a vertigo, depth opening upon depth, of the worst loneliness that he had ever experienced. He went quickly and fiercely into his room. Pigeon-toed, Sundar Singh stood furtively in front of the table, his hands behind his back.

Alan exploded. 'Get out! *Jao*!'

The boy cowered, his lips trembling. 'Sahib?'

Alan controlled himself. 'Go,' he said, with a gesture almost pleading. He forced himself to smile. '*Ram ram*,' he said.

When the boy had gone, Alan hurried towards the bed, but was trapped in the long looking-glass. He stared at himself, unwillingly.

'Peace be with you,' he said, aloud. His image mouthed back.

He turned out the light, and undressed in the dark. In the shrine of the white netting, his fingers moved, but confusedly; he seemed to own eleven of them. He placed his hands together, palm to palm, the fingers straight and still.

'Christ, let me out of this,' he said.

In the east, the dawn was green and tender, and the plain flowed towards it from their feet. Above them the stars, weakened and shrunken, hung more recognisably than usual in the great dome of the Indian sky.

'Holl,' said Alan, 'you're weakening. You're getting soft.' The horse that confronted him had a saddle on it.

Holl grinned raggedly, and, almost abashed, ran his hand through his downy hair. 'Giddy-up,' he said. 'We're going to bash the guts out of these poor old mokes.'

They moved off sedately, at a walk, side by side.

Holl coughed. 'Did I talk a lot of crap last night?'

Alan was wondering when he was going to fall off, but the stirrups were a comfort. 'Yes,' he said.

'What about?'

'You,' said Alan, more cheerfully; his horse seemed almost malleable. 'You, and victor-ee. It seems you are going to win the war. You personally.'

Holl groaned. 'It was that sodding barman. He let me have half a bottle of whisky, for cash. I'll have to see that the Mess President sacks him. God, I might have done anything. *Anything*!'

'You also ran through the seduction of the housemaster's daughter, your career in the garage and in the ring.'

Holl was making nervous flapping gestures with his free hand, and swearing under his breath. He reined in his horse. 'Alan!' he said.

Enchanted, Alan found that his own horse too could be stopped. 'Yes?'

Holl swallowed, and said with reluctance: 'Actually, it wasn't the housemaster's daughter.'

'Oh?'

'Her father ran the local sweet-and-tobacco shop.' Holl looked miserable. 'I'm sorry.'

He looked anxiously at Alan, and then saw that he was laughing. His face cleared, and suddenly he began to laugh too, boisterous and forgiven. He kicked his horse into a trot and Alan's followed.

'Sit forward!' shouted Holl.

Alan's horse was throwing him around in the saddle.

'Rise! rise in your saddle, lump!' cried Holl. 'All right, canter, then.'

The tumult yielded to a smooth, immensely powerful rocking motion. Alan got his balance, and began to enjoy himself.

'O.K.,' shouted Holl. 'Let 'em rip!'

The tempo changed again, and the horse was going much faster than Alan felt to be safe.

'Go with her! Just go!' cried Holl over his shoulder, already yards in front.

Alan shut his eyes, and went with her. Presently, finding himself still horse-borne, he opened his eyes. He found himself devouring distance as though he starved for it. The air rushed smooth and cool in his temples; the thunder of his progress was triumphal and the brown earth shuddered at his passing. He opened his mouth and shouted, and felt the sound snatched from his mouth by the speed. Confusedly, he wondered why he had been missing this all these years, and then thought that now he had found it, it could well go on forever.

In fact it stopped rather abruptly at the edge of a small mud village. Alan found himself clutching his horse round its neck. When he had righted himself, he turned, sweating and shining, to Holl. He spoke with solemnity. 'That's the most wonderful sensation I've ever had. Let's do it some more.'

But Holl was thirsty. They dismounted by the village shop, a hovel with brilliantly coloured bottles stacked outside on wooden crates, and an array of sweets and cakes covered with flies. They drank saccharine-sweet fizzy lemonade, sitting under a starveling tree and looking at the village, while a small crowd of naked pot-bellied children looked at them.

'You've good hands,' Holl said, appraising. He looked at Alan and grinned, warm and open.

'Lord!' said Alan. 'It's bloody marvellous.' He smiled back at Holl, and stretched luxuriously. Relaxed, he seemed to float.

'Only one better feeling in the world,' Holl said, sucking. 'And that's a woman. Why, I remember at college – I used to play rugger for the town – Saturdays, you know, a good game, and then a soak in a piping hot bath, and out to the pub. That's when a man's really relaxed, and after a couple of beers it just comes bubbling up. There's no holding it.' He shook his bottle meditatively, and the bright yellow liquid fizzed. 'Women,' he said, with regret, and drank to them. 'That's life. That's *living*.' He belched. 'That's bloody *poetry*.'

'Maybe I don't play enough rugger.' Alan was prepared to concede a point. He hadn't thought about Lettice in quite those terms. He tried to remember her as she stood in the firelight, wearing only her hair and a soft bloom like that of a ripe peach on the stem, but his eye was caught by a flowering of rich purple and orange at the entrance of a hut twenty-five yards away. The vivid colour swirled, and, rising, settled slender and flowing about the upright figure of a woman. She moved towards them, floating in the sun beneath the earthen pot she carried on her head, and the subtle, consummately poised balance of her movement bewitched him with the flattery of music in the veins, so that for a second his breath caught in his throat.

With unwary joy, he exclaimed to Holl, that that was why he had volunteered for service in India.

Uncomprehending, Holl looked at the woman. She passed them indifferently, without a glance. Holl said it was shocking the way Indians treated their women.

Alan thought of trying to explain. His father was a Civil Servant, who served state and family with equal selfless devotion; only recently had Alan decided that this devotion, while admirable, was grey, and that his father was a victim. When, enhanced by scholarships, yet still costing his father far more than could decently be afforded, he had gone up to Cambridge, his father had said, liberally, that the great thing at the university was to meet people and talk to them; but he added, as rider, that it was also a good thing to get a first, for then, armoured, one could make one's choice. 'Because,' said his father, 'if you then pass high enough into the Civil Service, you can choose; everything is open to you: Treasury, Education, what you like, even Foreign Service can be managed nowadays without a private income – anything...' At the time this seemed reasonable enough, but already, by the end of his first term, it had become clear to Alan that 'anything' could not be confined within the opportunities offered by the Civil Service; there were other ways of life.

By the end of his first year, he had plumped for professional scholarship; he would be a don. Dons seemed civilised, to own an extraordinary freedom, and to have enough money to get by quite handsomely; scholarship offered endless vistas, exciting yet agreeably secure, to curiosity, and as he was reading languages, travel would be a necessity though all the time he would have a sound home base to work from. But when, at the beginning of his third year, war broke, it was as if he saw Cambridge from a bomber; like a suddenly exposed ants' nest it lay open to hostile skies, scurrying with minute and flustered academics, impotent and almost frivolous in their irrelevance. He had no choice now; he must be a soldier, but he would not go back to Cambridge when it was all over. He knew, he thought, about war; it was a job to be done. His father had done it before him, but his father had started with illusions and had in consequence to become disillusioned; Alan's advantage, it seemed to him, was that he started with no illusions and therefore could not be disillusioned. Determined to believe nothing that anyone might say, to commit his soul to no cause, and (intellectually, at least) resigned to death if he should prove unlucky, he set about war; he would be as efficient a soldier as it lay in his power to be, because that was the job in hand, but also he would get anything out of war that war might, in its large way, turn up in his path. A free trip to India, when offered, suited him perfectly, and though he had not expected moments of enlightenment to kindle from, for example, a ride on a horse and a woman in a purple sari, he was open to accepting these moments wherever they might spring from.

But what Alan actually said to Holl was: 'It's a very exciting country, if you've never been outside Europe before. It's a very beautiful country, and I might never get another chance to see it if I go back to Cambridge after the war and teach the boys and girls French and German.'

Holl sucked, and said: 'That woman obviously had trachoma.' Then with some warmth, he added: 'Can't see what you see in it. Nasty dirty unhygienic superstitious lying bribing bunch of bastards.'

Alan asked why, in that case, Holl had come to India.

'You may well ask. Except that I'd blotted my copybook at home, and it seemed a good idea to try somewhere else when the Army offered it free. In fact, there are two advantages in this benighted country: I might stick on here when it's all over and wangle into the police or something like that. You get responsibility out here much earlier; I mean there are men of my age, twenty-eight or so, who have hundreds of men under their command and hundreds, thousands of square miles of which they're little kings. I don't say I'd mind that. And then you can live like a gentleman – you *have* to live like a gentleman, what with sweepers and cooks and bearers; no domestic problem. And then horses are cheap or even free if you're near a Remount place like we are. Only drawback's the climate and the inhabitants.' He rose, swatting viciously at flies, and remounted his horse.

They rode back the way they had come, the sun now warm on their backs, and the wind of their speed astringent on their faces. Alan rode in a thoughtless serenity, that was not seriously disturbed when he fell off once, and then again.

They turned in at the gates of the camp, and Holl wove his horse between the dose-planted saplings along the camp road, in and out. He stopped in a little crowd of grinning troops, and dismounted amongst them, swearing gaily at them until their teeth threatened to fly out in the ecstasy of their mirth. Following sedately behind at a walk, Alan recognised the warm feeling in him as happiness; he surveyed the camp with affection and surprise; he felt at ease.

A hand caught at his stirrup. It was Sundar Singh. Alan understood that the adjutant wanted him, urgently. '*Jilo*, sahib,' said Sundar Singh, making flapping, chicken-like darts in the direction of the adjutant's office. 'There is a telegram. Priori-tee.'

Alan dismounted, and found his knees wobbling under him. He had to stand still for a moment before he could walk. That would of course be due to the strain on muscles unaccustomed to riding; but as he went across to the office he was preparing nervously for the announcement of disaster. A bomb on Lettice? On his parents?

The adjutant was out of temper; he had been aroused from his lie-in. 'Where the bloody hell have you been? I sent for you half an hour ago. There's a high-powered cable about you here from General Staff, Simla. They want to know: are you capable of instructing certain officers and N.C.O.s in German?'

'*What*?'

'Whether you are capable of instructing in German. That'll be for the new highly hush-hush parachute bodies, I take it. I think it's somewhere near Simla, and very nice too. Cool and sweet; thousands of dispossessed wives thrown in for good measure. I didn't know you knew German. Do you?'

'Yes,' said Alan, somewhat distrait. His imagination had caught. He saw himself, a B.A. gown fluttering black over khaki shorts, instructing on a dais before a submissive audience of strong brave men who watched his chalk respectfully as it wrote on the blackboard: *Ich bin ein Freund; bitte konnen-Sie mich ans nachste Power-station dirigieren; Ich muss es sofort aufblasen*. When they had learned that, off they would go in aeroplanes, while he started on the next batch. He must look up the German for 'power station.'

'Yes, I think I could manage that. I read German at Cambridge, and lived in Heidelberg for nine months.' He stared unseeing at the adjutant, who was brooding over the telegram and smoothing his moustache.

'Cushiest assignment I ever heard of,' said the adjutant. He looked up at Alan almost enviously. 'I wish I was hot on German. But

Scrapings will hit the ceiling pronto when he hears; subalterns come and go here as though it were an R.T.O.'s office. Either they're N.B.G. and we have to work like hell to wish them on to Brigade or some other safe coop, or else one of these weird mystic bodies stoops from Simla, and just pinches them without as much as a by-your-leave.'

Alan's mind rolled, luxurious as a water buffalo in mud. He could stop pretending to be an infantry officer; he could relax. In Simla, or wherever it was, there would be people interested in things that interested him; people with whom he could talk on subjects other than military. He would perhaps have time to read, time to explore, time to think. He would be safe, and honourably so.

He stood beside the adjutant, looking out of the window of the hut. The adjutant was talking but Alan did not hear what he said. He felt like singing. Then his eyes focused; he was looking at Holl who was still out there grinning like a tiger in a bunch of sepoys. He saw Holl fling his arms wide in a great, rich, prodigal gesture, his gold tooth sparkling like a shower of sovereigns. He heard distantly a roar resembling *whoosh*! And saw the sepoys scattering with distinctly informal salutes. Then Holl turned, and came striding towards the office in which they stood.

Alan was surprised to hear himself saying: 'Better just think it over, I suppose. I mean I don't have to go, do I? If my German wasn't good enough?'

The adjutant stared at him. 'Well. No. It's entirely your decision. It's up to you, you're the only person who knows.'

There was a silence. Alan saw Holl had stopped for a word with the subadar-major.

The adjutant said: 'Well, think it over. But let me know before tiffin. They'll be wanting the answer at the other end.'

As Alan went out, he brushed past Holl, and grinned rather feebly in answer to Holl's grin. He went on towards his room with his head singing in tingling falsetto: Hee-ar my prayer! The good Lord had heard; Alan's hands joined together as he walked, his fingers counting themselves all present and correct. Yet his body somehow dragged, almost stumbling, under his galloping mind; he tried to urge it on, to skip, to jump, even, but it would not respond, and he arrived at his room in such disorganisation that he tripped over the step and all but fell on to his bed.

He found Sundar Singh standing by him. He was as bashful as a virgin offering herself, simpering, his hands behind his back; then with an awkward flourish, he almost hit Alan in the face with a pair of brown boots, one in each hand. They shone like chestnuts fresh from the shell. Sundar Singh studied Alan's face anxiously.

'*Thik hai*, sahib?'

Alan gathered that his orderly was inquiring not only whether the boots were properly cleaned to his taste, but also whether the outcome of the telegram was satisfactory. He suppressed a groan, and inspected the boots. He said they were splendid; everything was splendid.

The orderly's face melted with pleasure, and the round body salaamed with happy reverence. He laid the boots like an offering at the foot of the bed, and went out.

'Now,' said Alan, aloud, 'think it over.' He turned on his back, and looked carefully at the fan revolving above him; it seemed to be having no effect whatever on the thickening heat of the day. Then it seemed as though it were revolving inside his head, in a perfect vacuum there established. There was anyway nothing to think over:

Entschieden ist die scharfe Schlacht,
Der Tag blickt siegend durch die Nacht.

It was decided. He would teach paratroopers or commandos German. Who said that? Schiller? or Goethe? Schiller, he thought.

He found he was wondering if the Mess would be empty. He decided there was a fair chance it would be, and went over, cautiously, unwilling to meet anyone. The dining-room proved in fact to be empty, and with a large relief he sat down and ate a healthy breakfast. Then, equally cautiously, he slipped out, and back to his room. Stretched on his bed once more, he looked at his watch. It was ten-fifteen. At eleven, he would step over to the adjutant and confirm his decision to go. No, he would go at ten-thirty; in a quarter of an hour's time.

In need of something to press against, he reached for the footboard of his bed, but there wasn't one. After turning about for some time, he looked at his watch again. It was ten-eighteen. He shook the watch, but it was going all right. A curious immobility invaded his limbs. It was very hot. The room seemed to be shrinking on him; outside all was quiet except for the distant creak of a bullock cart's wheel. Then someone hawked explosively under his window and spat. He found his shirt was wet through with sweat and realised that the fan had stopped.

'I must get up,' he said loudly to himself as if on a desert island, 'and take this shirt off. And tart up for the adjutant. And get the orderly to go find someone to fix the fan.'

He stayed where he was, stretched rigid as on a rack, the sweat running down into his eyes. He could hear his watch running along by his pillow, and beyond it, the slower pulse of his travelling clock, and beyond that a slow booming thud that was his heart. He wondered why he bothered to keep a watch and a clock going. It occurred to him, appalling, that no one had wound his heart up.

Some time, some ages later, when the door burst open and Holl came stamping in, Alan realised that this was what he had been waiting for.

Holl lumbered round the room, and back again, flicking glances at Alan out of the corners of the pale eyes. Then he sat on the edge of the table. He looked at Alan's books, and drummed his fingers on the table top. With some deliberation he lit a cigarette, and at last bent the eyes full on Alan. Alan did not know what he was expecting, except that it would be something loud. Still Holl did not speak, but Alan was surprised to feel that the eyes looked more wounded than anything else.

'So,' said Holl at last, very mild, 'you're to be a schoolmarm in Simla.'

He had changed from the corduroy slacks in which he rode into uniform khaki shirt and shorts. The winding of his ankle-puttees was mathematically correct, and from them his legs went up like trunks.

'Ah,' said Alan. His throat seemed dry. He cleared it, and said: 'I'll be rather good at it.'

'And I thought you were a soldier,' said Holl. His eyes now were puzzled, and his voice frankly grieving.

Alan leant sideways and took a cigarette. He lit a match. 'I am a devout coward,' he said, playing for dead-pan bravado. He looked not at Holl but at the match, and indeed the match was shaking in his fingers. Who said that? he thought. Certainly not Schiller. Perhaps Bob Hope. He could feel Holl looking at him, and could feel him standing off from him, bristling like a dog. He realised that his remark, however true, was, in this company, in poor taste; but his throat stuck, and he could think of no way of modifying it.

Holl stood there, bristling, and said nothing.

In desperation, Alan repeated: 'I'll be good at it, you see. Be some use.'

Holl made a noise something like a spit; then he rolled his shoulders as if loosening up, and heaved one arm half up in the familiar gesture that he used for getting his troops on the move; then the arm collapsed to his side. 'I dare say you will,' he said. 'I dare say.' He looked vacantly around; then he poked up at Alan's fan with his stick. 'Your fan needs fixing,' he said. Without looking at Alan again, he left the room.

As the door shut, Alan sat up convulsively, and hurled his cigarette against the wall. Then he had to get up, and stamp on it to put it out. He looked at his watch; it was almost eleven. He took off his shirt, and rubbed down with a towel. He put on a clean shirt, shorts, boots and puttees. He had seven shots at the puttees before they would fall more or less into place, and his temper rose as he fought them. He stood in front of the glass, hitched his shorts straight, and combed his hair; the face looked sweaty but otherwise unravaged – indeed it seemed rather smug. We must have the courage of our cowardice, it said.

'You boozing, brainless, fornicating, sentimental oaf!' cried Alan in despair to the absent Holl. Seizing cap and stick, he proceeded at a brisk mechanical march towards the adjutant's office. That afternoon he would write letters: to Lettice: *Darling, I have been chosen out as a schoolmarm...* to his parents: *You may be relieved to hear that...* and so they would, what with one son dead in the Middle East already.

The adjutant was talking to one of the company commanders about latrines. Alan saluted smartly, and waited, his mind as blank as the burning parade ground out on to which he looked.

There was, it seemed, to be an inspection shortly of latrines. 'For some reason,' the adjutant was saying, 'all officers who have served on the Northwest Frontier have got very fly-conscious.' He raised his eyebrows at Alan, and a brief hiatus in the conversation stood open. The two officers stood with their heads inclined slightly towards Alan, as though half pausing to allow a waiter to put something on a plate in front of them. In the top of Alan's head, a delicate counterpoised machinery began to work; a key seemed to turn, levers lifted gently, wheels turned over, and tumblers fell into place in a succession of muted, accurate clicks.

Already the adjutant was talking again, about fly-traps, but Alan's mouth had flown open, and it pronounced loudly but calmly:

'I have come to the conclusion, sir, that my German really isn't good enough.'

'One maggot and all hell's let loose,' said the adjutant. 'What was that, Alan?'

Alan swallowed and repeated his statement.

'Oh.' The adjutant scuffled among the papers on his desk, and found the telegram. With pencil poised, he talked some more about latrines to the company commander. Then he broke off in mid-sentence, looking faintly puzzled.

'Did you say you did *not* want to go to Simla?'

'Yes.'

'That's what I thought you said.' He looked at Alan, a question hovering unformulated under his eyebrows. Then, with a large blue pencil, he wrote NO on the telegram. The question faded, and he said, abstractedly: 'Ah well, it's your pigeon,' and went on talking to the company commander. 'Scrapings is bad enough without all this huroosh when it comes to what he calls the Disposal of Waste Matter, ha ha...'

Alan was walking back across the scorching dust to his room. He was dazed. For some reason, he was for the moment obsessed with a vision of the *munshi* who had taught him Urdu in the Cadet College and, who, towards the end of Alan's course, had been sacked after a row with the authorities. He had paid a mourning state visit to Alan to say goodbye; holding his bicycle, he had wept a good deal, maintaining with a genuine if rather watery dignity that there had been a conspiracy against him, because he was known to disbelieve in the efficacy of war, let alone its morality; nevertheless, he had said as he left, snuffling: 'Right will prevail; God will turn the blind men's eyes to the truth.'

A raucous shout shattered this vision. 'Are you *deaf*?' the adjutant was bellowing from his doorway. 'Come back a moment. I almost forgot to tell you. Your place in the Signals Course at Poona has come through; you'll be taking that up now you're not going to Simla.'

Alan saluted, and started on his way again. The news was of no significance.

'For heaven's sake, stand still for one second! The course starts *tomorrow*, so you'll have to get weaving. You can get on a train and clock in at Poona tonight; you take your orderly with you. I'll get the railway warrants fixed and you pick 'em up at the office this afternoon.'

'Yes, sir,' said Alan, and started off again.

In his room, he stood. His eyes wavered stupidly over his worldly possessions; he would have to pack them, he would have to resolve the problem of which to take and which to leave. Overcome by the necessity of organisation, he sat down feebly at the table. Beside his portable typewriter stood a dummy Morse buzzer; he began to tap on it.

'Bz bz,' he said; and then, faster: 'Bz bz bz. Berz berz berz. Bz...'

After a little the message became coherent; he was sending out SOS signals. Dropping the key, he rose, and faced his baggage. Presently Sundar Singh appeared; the boy seemed half-appalled and half-overjoyed at the prospect of going to Poona. After they had packed and unpacked and repacked a few times, Alan thought he would not go into the Mess for tiffin. Instead, he sent Sundar Singh down to the lines to fetch him some troops' curry and chapattis. He ate walking up and down his room, and as he walked it seemed to him that he was beginning to disintegrate like a ship broken down in a heavy sea. It became imperative to drop anchor, or at least to make some pretence at dropping anchor, even if only to trail overboard an empty cable. He sat down, and took pen and ink and paper; to begin with his hand rested impotently on the paper, and when he lifted it, the paper stuck to it and rose with it. He took a fresh piece of paper, focused upon it, and quickly, briefly – indeed, almost tersely – dictated to his hand a proposal of marriage to Lettice. And so having set his course, he took an aspirin, lay down and went to sleep.

At four o'clock Sundar Singh woke him, and they set off in a truck to the station. As they stood waiting for the train to leave, there was some shouting from the entrance to the platform, and a moment later Holl came heaving down towards them.

Holl was radiant, and stertorous. 'Thought I'd miss you. Only got back to camp twenty minutes ago from town.' His right arm came up and over. Wincing, Alan took the hearty clap on his shoulders.

'That's a boy!' shouted Holl. 'Uh knew you didn't really mean it. You'll be with us in Ceylon.'

Alan jumped. 'Ceylon?'

Holl roared. 'Met old Stuffins from Brigade at the Club. He swears we're going to Ceylon. Bloody garrison duties for the duration. Mark you, Stuffins is imbecile, but then so is G.H.Q., so what d'you know?' Alan felt winded, and wished to grapple with this announcement which seemed unworthy, but Holl had already passed to the subject of Poona, where, he said, the girls were good; might get over one Sunday himself. Then he stopped and peered at Alan.

'You know you shouldn't –' he said, and stopped. He looked embarrassed, and his high cheekbones shone in the late sun. In a low voice he started again: 'That stuff about –'

'Devout cowardice,' said Alan.

It was Holl who winced. 'You don't want to say things like that,' he said earnestly and visibly distressed. 'It gets around. Loose talk, and all that. I mean, it's not as if you meant it?' The query hung in the air, and the train's whistle snatched it up and pierced the sky with it.

Sundar Singh was plucking at Alan; the train was about to leave. Alan climbed up and in, and slammed the door; through the open window he leaned out over Holl. With his mouth open, Holl looked back up at him; foreshortened, his face appeared to register agony.

'All right,' said Alan snappishly. 'No. Of course not. It was just a crack.' He bared his teeth. 'Ha ha.'

'Ha ha!' echoed Holl enormously. Agony passed over and he became a bumpkin split with laughter.

'Blast you,' said Alan.

He stayed looking out of the window as Holl dwindled. Small cinders rushed against the side of his face. The train gathered speed; Holl was small now on the platform, dwindling rapidly, but he seemed to be waving a big khaki handkerchief. Disgusted, Alan withdrew his head and shut the window.

TWO

POONA, and the Signals Course, proved agreeably gentle after life in the battalion; almost academic. True, the work was intensive, but Alan found it intriguing and within his abilities, and it was enlivened for him by the presence of George Baynes, with whom for six months Alan had shared a room at the Cadet College. George's unit, according to him, was 'holding the north-west Marches of the Raj.'

'Or at least, we shall be very shortly. But we don't seem to have any troops yet; just a European cantonment and a bazaar. I spent all my first Sunday dropping cards on the mem-sahibs; sweetly Kipling – when we climb at length into those hideous hills it'll be even back to Henty. But I shall be out of it all before then; all the strings are pulling for me in Simla. I hope they're pulling for you? You never would take the necessary trouble about that sort of thing, and it's so important.'

Alan felt himself blush. 'I dare say,' he said hurriedly, but he could feel George's eyes suspicious on him. 'I'm not so sure, *actually*, that I'd make a good staff officer.' He fluffed a bit.

'Heaven forbid! you don't want to be a staff officer. You want to be a back-room boy. Why, I've never seen anyone more back-room than you, Alan. The first-floor back may have passed, but you're up there in the rear attics, a natural. You can't help it.'

Alan changed the subject, and soon after left the Mess, where he had met George, and went back to his room. He had been allotted a large apartment, almost luxurious in its large bare airiness; it was on the first floor of a long, low, whitewashed building, and gave on to a balcony running the whole length of the building. He climbed the stairs to the balcony, found his door, and then discovered that it was blocked by a large bundle strewn across the threshold. This proved to be Sundar Singh, fast asleep.

Alan roused him. 'What are you doing here?'

Sundar Singh, sleep-hazy, rose to humble attention, and said that he was sleeping there.

Alan was annoyed; he had spent some time earlier that night in fixing up his orderly's accommodation in the Indian lines provided for that purpose. He said so.

Sundar Singh stood where he was. After some pressure, he said, almost fiercely, that he did not wish to sleep in the lines; the lines, he said, were full of riff-raff like pioneers, R.I.A.S.C., clerks – people virtually no better than sweepers. The lines were no place for a fighting soldier.

Alan was astounded, but also touched. Gently, he said that he was afraid Sundar Singh must go back there. The orderly did not budge.

'*Hukm hai*!' said Alan, firmly. 'It is an order.'

Rather to his surprise, this phrase moved the boy, and he went off slowly down the balcony.

'Well, I'm damned!' said Alan, to himself. God-like, one snapped one's fingers, and these strange creatures obeyed. It wasn't right; it was not at all right. One had absolutely no justification to take advantage of them like that.

He went to bed, and lay in the hot dark, snapping his fingers in all directions. He was confused. There was that boy claiming to be a fighting soldier, refusing to associate with low-caste clerks but quite happy to spend his days cleaning Alan's boots. Alan himself had that very morning lodged a claim with destiny to be considered as a fighting soldier; open up the bloody battlefields, he had said. But destiny had clearly instantaneously decided that he was not of that caliber and had replaced the vision of desert battle with the coral island of Ceylon, implying that it found him faintly absurd. As a fighting soldier, he had also taken the decision to marry Lettice; as one possibly about to die, he had pledged his troth, and now he was not about to die at all. He felt that he had deceived Lettice with false pretences and began to wish that he had not posted the letter. But, even more keenly, he felt that he had been let down on all sides. He tried to think of Lettice, to reassure her that, though he might have misled her, he loved her still, he needed her; but Lettice, on the other side of the world, was elusive. His need boxed vainly against an amorphous absence. He started to thrash in his sheets and lost his pillow; groping for it on the floor, he became ensnared in the ends of the mosquito net, and had to fight his way out. Bewildered and resentful, he crouched by his bed, and then groped his way for a drink of water. Before he got back into bed, on a sudden impulse, he opened his door.

Sundar Singh lay prone across the threshold, pretending to be asleep.

Alan stood looking at him. 'I won't have it,' he thought, but feebly. The boy looked as unanswerable as a corpse, cold in the moonlight on the concrete. A long black bar of shadow from the pillar of the balcony fell across his body. 'I won't have it,' thought Alan, and closed the door very gently upon Sundar Singh, and got back into bed. He was thinking of Irma, now dead. Irma had been a large mongrel with a strong strain of sheepdog whom he had owned when a boy; she used to sleep across his door, because his mother would not allow her to sleep in the room with Alan (unhygienic, she used to say). It had been a comfortable feeling, he remembered, sleeping with the dog outside his door. He fell asleep.

One evening later in the first week of the course, Alan went with George to a cinema in the town. The film was called *Blood and Sand*, and was rather boring, while the cinema was hot. In the gallery sat the white military, sweating in their khaki, with their women; in the pit, explosive with snuffling and coughing and sporadic loud conversations in Hindi, sat mostly Indians. When the film at last was ended, the King-Emperor looked forth sadly and seriously from the screen out of a fluttering Union Jack. The gallery rose and stood correctly to attention, thumbs to seams, looking down at the Indians who were filing out beneath them noisily.

Alan and George returned to the school in a horse-tonga.

'The sooner Simla pulls me out of this, the better,' said George. 'There's something very improper about being in command of Indians. It's funny how you can't realise that the old cliché about the White Man's Burden isn't a joke until you actually come to India. Every time an Indian does something I tell him to do, I feel I've lost another thousand years or so of Paradise. Yet I'm not a religious man.'

'Well, I don't know,' said Alan, though in theory he agreed entirely with George, or had done, until very recently.

'Come, come, Alan. Are you getting corrupted?'

'Not at all!' said Alan with some heat, and launched with some heat, though vaguely, into a discourse on the Necessity of the Historical Situation.

Eventually, with a glint of glasses in his shadowy corner of the jingling tonga, George suggested that Alan was talking drivel.

Stung into direct statement, Alan said: 'Maybe it's illogical, but once one *is* in command, I don't see that you ought to let them down.'

George received this in shocked silence. Then he cleared his throat, patted Alan on the knee, and courteously if overtly changed the subject; it was, he said, academic anyway. He had a theory: the war would be over within the year. Now that Russia appeared at last to be holding the Nazi advance, and we seemed to be doing a little better in the Middle East – at any moment now, in George's opinion, the United States would realise they'd better get in to qualify for loot of victory. Why, said George, even the Irish Free State would be in there fighting before long. 'It is now November, 1941. I'll bet you sixpence we'll be eating Christmas dinner in Berlin next year. Until that happy time, let survival be our watchword. I believe in personal survival before death. By all means let us put our shoulders to the wheel, for it is certainly a fairer, rounder, more righteous wheel than the enemy's wheel, quite apart from the fact that we have a vested interest in our wheel continuing to roll on –

'But let others do the dirty work for us!' said Alan.

'Don't be disingenuous,' said George with severity. 'You don't empty your own dustbins, do you? To every man his proper trade. War calls for millions of manual workers, but if you are, by nature, breeding and training a brain-worker, you owe it to yourself and even more to society to work at that which you are best at. Just because "intellectual" is a popular term of abuse, one is not justified in denying it, nor is one justified in pretending to be a labourer when one isn't any good at labouring. Morally, it's wrong; worse, it's criminally inefficient.'

The tonga had stopped. They climbed out. After some argument with the driver, Alan arrived at a compromise about the fare.

'You paid him too much,' stated George, yawning.

'I paid going, too.'

'That's right,' said George. 'Have you got anything to drink up in your room?'

'Only limes.'

'Good. Let's go and have some. I'll come up.'

They climbed up to the balcony.

'Good God!' said George, jumping as if for snakes. 'What's that?'

Sundar Singh rose to his full height of five foot two, and greeted Alan. They went in past him, and shut the door.

'I like that,' said George. 'Against my principles, but splendidly feudal. We still have bearers; you wouldn't catch mine sleeping on guard over his lord and master, he's far too grand. He was once nearly a bearer to Wavell when Wavell was a subaltern, and he goes around in glory like a strip-cartoon character with a permanent balloon fixed on his mouth, inscribed *Failed bearer to Lord Wavell Sahib*. He thinks I'm terrible trash and he steals all my handkerchiefs.'

Stretched in the only armchair, with a toothglass full of tepid lime and water, he reverted to the theme of inefficiency. His short body was as precise and perky as a bird's, even when he relaxed; he was darker still than Alan, with a very pale skin, and mild but slightly incredulous popping grey eyes which his spectacles from time to time would fire with an oddly bellicose flash. His short black hair capped him like a penguin's head-feathers.

Alan wished George would go away, for on this subject he spoke from a position of unfair authority, because, on his left breast, neatly clad in cellophane, shone the coloured ribbon of the D.C.M. He had been a bombardier at Dunkirk, and there had been guilty, as he would explain with ready affectation, of taking an uncalculated risk and of displaying gallantry. In fact he had conducted a brisk but quite extensive tour well in front of his own lines, solo in a carrier, collecting up wounded. 'It was a grave error,' he would explain. 'I understood that I was being covered by machine guns; it was only when I got back that I found out that they were German machine guns, hostile rather than friendly. I'd lost my spectacles and couldn't really see.' The ribbon, however, was undeniably useful; at the Cadet College, he had used it constantly to subdue what he believed to be the arrogance of the staff, very few of whom had seen action in modern warfare; pigeon-pouting like a film star, George had on occasions even quelled the bombast of the brigadier's bosom, numerically far superior in ribbons, but rather old-fashioned ones, a war or so old.

Now he had fixed Alan with a primly needling stare. 'You want to be very careful. If your unit's actually standing by, to all intents and purposes, to proceed overseas, it may all happen with a nasty abrupt suddenness. And once you're overseas, it's much harder to get back.'

Alan looked at him glumly, and said nothing.

'You're not your usual chatty self,' said George. He rose, yawning. 'Time for bed.'

But as the course proceeded in the hot, but not too hot, November sun, Alan became less glum. Over the dry brown countryside, they ran out telephone wires and linked imaginary detachments of troops one with the other. On the abrupt hills that strewed the landscape like a stranded herd of leviathan, they flipped messages through the clear air on winking heliographs. It was positively agreeable. Like beetles with long wavering steel antennae, they promenaded gravely with walkie-talkie wireless sets strapped to their backs. Admittedly for the first few days the relative slackening of tension, compared with the tenseness of the battalion, had fostered in Alan an unease that was almost guilty; but this subsided, and with it a cloud seemed to pass from his days. It was as though he had been reprieved, and on the far horizon stretched Ceylon, no longer an absurdity, an insult, but a coral strand in the Indian Ocean. The clash of Russian and German armour stretched north and south across Europe in the battle for Moscow; the sand-clouded turmoil in North Africa round Tobruk; these intruded only in the morning newspaper like news from another planet. For an hour a day he sat in his room with an elderly, grizzled *munshi*, talking in Urdu of this and that, but his evenings were usually free. He talked endlessly with George about non-military matters. He tried to talk with Sundar Singh, but his orderly remained secretive, apparently largely because descriptive language was beyond his experience in any tongue. Alan established that his orderly was in fact seventeen years old (though he subsequently retracted this and swore he was eighteen); that he was married and had one child, but no good as it was a daughter. That he had joined the Army because his family always joined the Army. His uncle was a havildar in the 2nd Battalion; his grandfather had been a subadar-major and was obviously a figure of paramount honour. His father was not spoken of; why, was not clear. Yet the boy's background remained for Alan entirely hazy; presumably it was a village much like those he sometimes passed through with George, as they walked in the cool dark beyond the school: a tight-packed agglomeration of squat mud huts, defined by their blackness deeper than that of the night, with chinks of yellow light showing as they approached, and then the almost substantial smell – burning cow dung, close-packed human bodies, cattle, urine, dust, flowers – and the spatter of voices and the huffing breath of oxen asleep.

Under questioning, Sundar Singh became quickly restive, turning his eyes from side to side as if seeking escape. Yes, he said; or: No. In the end, Alan gave up with the feeling that he had been prying improperly, though the boy's uniform seemed all the more certainly a disguise. Once he thought he had caught him. An hour after lunch with the *munshi*, he came quickly, rather late, out of his room on his way to the afternoon parade. It was very hot, and a blazing sun turned the concrete steps down from the balcony into solid blocks of gold, and his steel-heeled boots went down the steps as though they were a xylophone, into the stillness of the afternoon. At the bottom, he had to wait to let a platoon of Punjabis go past; slow and deliberate the soldiers marched, more like gorillas than men, but huge-headed in their turbans; long arms swung crooked at the elbow, bony knees jerked outwards, and on their heels their black shadows mimed every movement. They went past, and beyond them, as though a curtain had been drawn, was revealed a plump Indian boy. Naked except for his snowy dhoti, he lay with one leg drawn up, yet as if floating, white and supple brown, in the calm and profound shadow of a great tree. Beyond him, in the sunlight, the stark buildings of the school stood solid and desolate in their shape of sun and shade, empty as if they had been abandoned for centuries. As Alan stood there, incomprehensibly bewitched, the afternoon seemed to congeal, and to contract breathless in fear of thunder.

But it was Alan's voice that crackled, oddly high, on the silence.

'Sundar Singh!'

A face, foreshortened, looked up towards him over a roll of chins. As Alan took a menacing step towards it, the brown and white figure sprang to its feet and fled with astonishing speed.

That evening, when Alan asked Sundar Singh what he had been doing there lying in a dhoti, and why he had not come when called, the orderly denied indignantly that he had been anywhere near that afternoon. 'It was somebody else. If I had been there, I would have come when you called, sahib. I always come. *Always*.' He looked very distressed, and suddenly Alan was unsure that it had been his orderly, and then profoundly shocked that he might not be able to tell one Indian from another.

Yet that, though it remained undigested and uncomfortable and disproportionately disquieting in his memory, was but a small incident. He was far more concerned with Lettice, about whom he thought a great deal, especially in her capacity of the woman he was going to marry. He examined her from all angles, and found her satisfactory. She was his anchor, and easily he swung about her; there was no doubt about it, being engaged was a great stabiliser; it gave a man a future and it gave him a centre. That Lettice might not accept his proposal had of course occurred to him, but the doubt did not begin to infect him, really to chill him, until, one Sunday, he realised that the end of the course was almost in sight. The feeling started with a slight, lonely, sickish arching of the stomach before dinner.

'In less than two weeks,' George had said, brooding over his third lime juice (for he did not drink), 'I shall be in a grit-laden, sweating, stopping train on my way to the Northwest Frontier.'

'What about Simla?' said Alan, tiresomely.

George looked peevish. 'Maybe the strings have got a bit tangled – perhaps too many people, pulling too hard and too often. It'll sort itself out.' He took a long swig, and cheered up. 'I tell you what,' he said with a debonair, devilish air, 'I bet you sixpence I get a cable from G.H.Q. demanding my immediate presence to succour the war-effort before this course is out.'

'That'll add up to a bob,' said Alan, 'when we don't have

Christmas in Berlin next year; you must learn to live within your income.' But he was thinking: less than two weeks more. He thought it with alarm; it would be precisely like going back to school had always been. He thought of the holiday tasks he had not carried out: he had made a vow to ride as often as possible and he had not taken out a horse once. Hurriedly, he switched his mind to easier topics; he contemplated Lettice. But it was at this point that he realised, in his heart, that Lettice had not answered his letter of proposal of marriage. He had written airmail at great expense. Not that that meant anything, of course: it might have been shot down; it might, as he suspected often happened, have gone by sea and be still rolling up the west coast of Africa in convoy, if not sunk. But he did not really believe any of that; it was an unpleasant shock. He realised that Lettice had had the letter; he knew it in his bones. He realised that she had not sent a telegram in answer. He could of course have wired the proposal in the first place, but the idea of such decisive intimacy expressed in capitals and doubtless with laughable misprints before the salacious eyes of post office officials would not for a moment have been tolerable to Alan. But she on the other hand, could easily have wired *Yes*. Whereas, equally obviously, being a girl of delicacy, of compassion: she could scarcely have wired a bleak *No*. If she meant No, she would write it, wrapped in sugar to make it more palatable. Even so, her letter would be about due; in fact, according to Alan's mental arithmetic, overdue.

He shifted in his creaking basket-chair, and shouted loudly for more whisky. He felt cold.

And then, one bright morning, he was on one of the bumpy hills beyond Poona, flashing away on one of the last exercises of the course. The heliograph was his favourite toy; the idea of harnessing the sun itself to the dispatch of absurd messages on a pocket-size mirror appealed to him. Also, on this occasion, he had discovered that George was his opposite number, three-quarters of a mile away; it pleased him to work so fast that George could not read it and had to plead for repeats, for in this manual skill he was superior to George. He had baffled George at least twice already that morning, and established a firm moral ascendancy, and he was sitting idly on his haunches, watching George's mirror stutter out a message about D Company withdrawing, when the sharp blink of concentrated sun fell silent. He waited a little then picked up his field-glasses. At George's end there appeared to be some sort of conference going on. Then the helio spluttered joyously, and Alan spelled out I WIN; a flicker followed, and then, with slow and stately pomp: LO I AM TRANSLATED. Through his field-glasses, Alan saw George with an orderly withdraw from the field of battle, presumably to Simla.

It was a very hot morning, and the sweat was sore under his chin, but, as he put down the glasses, he felt again that cold and lonely ache of departures. It seemed a very long time before the exercise was over, and they arrived back at the school. He threw his topee on the bed, splashed his face with cold water, and was just going out to find George, when he saw a note on his table. It was from the post office, and it said: *Sir, kindly callover to this Office for Regd letter. I have eet.*

The cold arch in his stomach swelled, and threatened capsizal. What was eet? The word NO formed like an expanding bladder in his mouth as he hurried to the post office, almost choking him. At the door he ran into George, who clutched him. He was looking smug but slightly ruffled.

'You owe me sixpence,' said George earnestly. 'I'll settle for eight annas.'

Fumbling, anxious to get past him, Alan paid up. 'A.D.C. to the Viceroy?'

George stood squarely in the doorway, blocking it; clearly he wished to talk. 'Alas! no. Funny business. General Staff Simla want to know if I'm capable of teaching certain officers and N.C.O.s German. Paratroops or commandos, I suppose. Not *quite* what I was expecting, I must admit, but trust the Army to cock it all up. And anyway, it's a foot in the door; only be there a month or two, then press on for better things.'

Alan was groaning as if George had hit him in the stomach. Then his voice squeaked: 'But you don't *know* German!'

'Oh, I say,' protested George. 'That's going a bit far. *Ich hab' eine tiefe Sehnsucht nach Dir*, and so on. I can get around in the country. Enough to be able to keep one step ahead of the boys in the crib, provided only that none of these certain officers and N.C.O.s are beastly little know-alls. I'll get by. Though really, of course, it's a job for you rather than for me, old boy.' He looked with compassionate concern at Alan from a safe height; then he had an idea. 'I might be able to wangle you in, how about that? What's the matter?'

The sweat ran down Alan's face. His mouth opened and shut. At length he said: 'You're not really going to accept'.'

'But of course. I've just cabled my adjutant to hurry things up as much as possible. The office here has agreed that I must leave at once. So I'll just be popping back to my unit to get things sorted out back there and hand over and pack and say goodbye. They say the confirming order, now they know that I'm a fine capable double *deutsch* officer *sprecher*, will be through in no time. You look rather queer. Are you all right?'

Alan's mouth was open for a vast desolate howl. Stiffly, he swallowed it. He managed a wan smile. 'Just jealous.'

'Why!' said George, rattling annas in his hand, 'never fret, boy. I'll be in there pulling strings in Simla for you. I'll have you there inside a few weeks, and you can crib for me. Now I'm afraid I must push back to the office. See you before I go.'

Alan went into the post office, and held on to the counter.

'Sir?' said the Eurasian clerk superciliously, shuffling papers indifferently from one pigeon-hole to another.

Alan rallied. 'You have eet,' he said, dully.

'Sir!'

'Sorry. You've a registered letter for me. Mr. Mart.'

The clerk shuffled vaguely at various pigeon-holes. Then he asked Alan if he was sure that there was a registered letter for him.

Alan battled with the huge NO ballooning again in his mouth. 'For God's sake, man! You sent me a note to say you had it.'

The clerk looked both insulted and bored, and turned his back on Alan. White alpaca-covered shoulders shrugged, suggesting that a second-lieutenant should know better than to waste a busy official's time.

'Well?' said Alan, rudely, as the back roved up and down the pigeon-holes.

At last the clerk turned. 'Packet. *Pack-utt*. Not letter,' he said with cold scorn, and held out a cardboard tube to Alan. 'There is also four annas to pay.'

Inside the tube was a rather ornate calligraphic scroll. Alan gathered that in his absence he had become a Bachelor of Arts (Cantab.).

That night, he saw George off. It was a painful procedure, but fortunately George had by now recovered fully his buoyancy; his head shone sleekly, blackly, in the station lights, and he spoke affectionately to Alan without stopping, mainly in Italian with a few German expressions thrown in. Presently the train steamed out. Alan went back to his room, which seemed very large and even more empty than it was large. He walked round it two or three times; it was like walking round a desert. Presently he located a loud ticking as his travelling clock, and knew it was time he went over to the Mess and had a drink.

The next day was Sunday, and on it the Japanese let loose on Pearl Harbour and upon Malaya. Alan was, like everyone else, shocked by this series of catastrophes, but also in a way stiffened by the news; as though, the light having fused in his own room, he had opened the door to find the whole world was dark too; at least everyone was in the dark together. He had in fact, in common with many other people, had much the same reaction at the time of Dunkirk, and again when Germany started to roll up Russia. He was willing to stand shoulder to shoulder with anyone; only, as on the Monday evening when he went down to the Mess, there wasn't anyone there to stand shoulder to shoulder with. So he sat there, with a paper, looking at a map of the Pacific and the Far East, discovering for the first time that, big though India was, it seemed to abut on territory very vulnerable to the Japanese. He put down the paper and was about to complain of the lack of light, when he realised that a black-out was in force. At last a fellow-officer came in, an Indian, and dropped into a chair opposite Alan, who studied him furtively. He was slender, light-complexioned, and wore his khaki with an impeccable precision that Europeans too could achieve, but also with a feline elegance that no European commanded. Alan always felt obliged to make conversation with Indian King's commissioned officers, terrified lest they should interpret silence as standoffishness. It always made him nervous, so that he usually overplayed his geniality. He was about to offer the Indian a cigarette, when he remembered that he did not smoke. Blushing for this gaffe, he caught back his gesture in mid-air, and said instead: 'D'you mind if I smoke?'

The Indian raised his eyebrows in astonishment, smiled in dazzling white amusement, and said: 'But my dear fellow!'

Alan said it was a nasty business about the Japanese.

His companion agreed that it was a nasty business. Obviously, he wanted to study the paper in peace, but Alan kept doggedly on. The conversation developed as such conversations usually did: the Indian presenting an affable but blank wall against which Alan, as though playing squash against himself, knocked up; every now and then, in spite of the greatest care, he would overhit, and find himself chasing like mad to keep the ball from going out of play. The rally was concluded abruptly but mercifully as the Indian rose. 'I'm so sorry,' he said, 'but I really must be getting along. I have a dinner engagement.'

'Oh,' said Alan, much relieved; too relieved, he gushed. 'I was hoping that – ' He stopped even more abruptly than the Indian had risen.

Inquiringly, his colleague looked at him, and then, as Alan failed to manage to say anything at all, he said: 'Well, good night.'

When he had gone, Alan got a large peg of whisky. It slid about in his sweating hand, and he had to put it down on the table. He had been going to ask the Indian to dine with him at the Club, forgetting not merely that he himself was not a member of the Club, but more important, that, as any lout knew, Indians were not *persona grata* at the Club. It was for precisely that reason that Alan had not joined it, on principle.

The Mess was sepulchrally empty once more. At last, another officer appeared; not one of the people that Alan had got to know and like during the course – indeed, rather, the reverse – but at least a European.

'My God!' said this officer, speaking generally. 'Those bloody little yellow Nips!' He shouted for a whisky. He was a fattish, fortyish man, very red, and, even at this early hour of the evening, sweating darkly through his khaki drill jacket at the armpits. He was a former business man from Calcutta, and held opinions. He looked far too old for the single pips that shone newly on his shoulders.

'They really are in Malaya,' he said. 'I can hardly believe it. But, by God! they'll find they've bitten off more than they can chew once those Yanks get moving.' He knocked back his whisky. 'Where the hell's all the crowd got to? I was thinking of stepping down to the Club for a bite. Care to join me?'

Alan started to refuse, and then was astonished to hear himself saying that indeed he would, thank you very much.

Over dinner, the stout man spoke in short staccato sentences, but with deep reverence, of the U.S. War Potential. Early in '39, it seemed, he had himself been in the States, in Cincinnati, Pittsburgh, Chicago, Detroit – oh, all over. 'We just don't know, in the Old Country' – his Scottish accent was fortified by the whisky – 'what Mass-Production means...' He wiped his lips after his coffee, and sighed, almost voluptuously. A fragment of over-bright tinned pea had strayed on to one of his cheeks, and bobbed with their sharp choppy rhythm as he talked. 'Mass-Production,' he said. 'But mind you, we mustn't underrate the Little Yellow Man. He's able; oh yes, don't you believe anyone who tells you different – he's able. But he just hasn't got the resources. Not got what it takes, not in the long run. No, no, old boy – this is on me.' He signed a chit with a flourish. 'The Sheer Weight of Armament that'll be rolling off those American belts! In a matter of months. Why, in a matter of weeks. Yes, sir!' The Scotch accent clashed with an odd American inflection.

In the bar they started on the whiskies again. It was gloomy, lit only by two candles, with little groups of men sunk in their own shadows and a dark hurrying murmur of talk.

'No need to *panic*,' said Alan's companion, looking disapproving at the candles. He panted slightly. 'Breath of air,' he said. But, on the veranda, it was quite dark, and seemed cold. The dined rotundity of the fat man's voice lost its brisk robustness on the blank night. 'What I mean is,' he was saying, 'got to do one's bit. Of course they tried to make out my business was a reserved occupation, but I told them... And I've always liked the Infantry, no nonsense about the Poor Bloody Infantry. Honest man's job. Of course, the M.O. said at first I was too old. Can you beat it? Too old!' He rolled the last words richly, but somehow the *o*'s merely faded like smoke-rings on the dark.

Alan was silent. The fat man creaked.

'If you'll excuse me a mo',' he said. 'I'll just try and get a call through to the wife. She's at Bombay, you know. Not a hope in hell with this flap on, I dare say. But I'll have a go, can't do any harm. She must be wondering.'

Alone, Alan sat forward in his chair. The black-out in fact, was far from complete once the eyes were used to the dark, flecked with lights, but nevertheless the night seemed the larger for it. The slightest of breezes moved across his face, and with it came from the trees a moan and a soft shore lap. It passed, but left his skin shrinking, and the vast arena of the night disturbed with the echoes of echoes. Memories stirred like the dead turning. Darkling plains, thought Alan, where ignorant armies clash by night. But really war was like being a railway station; people passed through you and were gone forever with the wild cry of trains, leaving only the old fish smell of Waterloo. He felt tears in his eyes, and turned indignantly to his whisky; he lay back in his chair, to see the more certain stars suspended, each one as if on its own string. But even as he stretched back, giddily he felt the earth beneath him, the whole Indian sub-continent tilt, actually lurch sideways into the ocean like a vast stricken aircraft carrier. He gripped the arms of his chair, and sat hurriedly erect; he reached for the whisky again, and then put it down untouched, for that's what it must be, too much whisky.

He sat forward again, and held his head safely in his hands, and waited for the fat man to reappear.

Two days later, before the Signals Course ended, Alan was recalled to his unit. The battalion was going overseas.

THREE

ALAN WAS PICKED UP from the Signals School by one of his battalion's 15-cwt trucks. He took over the wheel, and covered the eighty miles in under two hours, wondering, as he did so, what the hurry was. But as, with an exultant roar, he changed down to take the corner off the main road into the camp, and caught sight of the austerely orderly pattern of the long huts, he realised that this was not at all like coming back to school; it was more like coming home. He climbed down from the driver's seat, and strolled stiffly, in a hard-bitten proprietary manner, towards the adjutant's office. A platoon moving past gave him a smart eyes-right, and he accepted it as a matter of course, instead of looking round to find out who was being saluted.

The adjutant was installed behind a precarious-looking scree of papers, talking to the subadar-major, to Harold Hockey, one of the company commanders, and to two clerks simultaneously. He looked younger than ever, although his face was soggy with fatigue, and drops of moisture shone on his moustache. He allowed himself a smile and a jerk of relief as he caught sight of Alan.

'Thank God *something* has turned up, anyway; have a good course?'

'Well,' said Alan, judiciously, and was prepared to start a judicial and reasoned account of the course's virtues and failings, but the adjutant cut in:

'Did you bring the anti-tank rifles?'

That was what the truck had been sent to collect, rather than Alan.

'Thank God for that. Fine sight we'd have been, disembarking in a theatre of war with those bloody wooden dummies. And now you've come as well, we may even have some officers to take with us. Since you went off, let's see, we've lost the second-in-command to the 14th Battalion, now forming, and we've lost a very tidy proportion of our best N.C.O.s to the same quarter. We've acquired one subaltern Indian gentleman, as Transport Officer, but the M.O. appears to be a doubtful quantity as far as service overseas is concerned. The Officers' Mess has no cooks. Whole thing's a shambles.'

'Where are we going?'

The others looked at each other and roared with laughter.

'Where, where, Oh, tell me where!' said Harold Hockey. 'Nobody knows. According to Brigade, it's now Basra. According to Scrapings, who seems to have some divine source, it's still Ceylon. According to Sam Holl, we're going straight to blood and glory in Malaya or Burma.'

'Ah yes,' said the adjutant, 'and that's another casualty. Sam's in hospital with a dose of malaria, and the doctors say he won't be out for another ten days. By when, you can bet your bottom rupee, we'll be on the high seas. For wherever.'

'*Sam* in hospital,' said Alan, disbelieving. 'It's impossible!'

'Passed out,' said the adjutant. 'On parade, first thing. You should have seen Scrapings' whiskers go up like thunder 'cross the bay – but poor old Sam wasn't tight, just stiff with malaria. Now you'd better hop along and get yourself straight; all personal kit to be ready to travel to the Training Battalion. We're liable to move any time at twelve hours' notice.'

Walking back to his room, Alan felt abandoned. It was unthinkable that the battalion should sail without Holl; he did not see how the battalion could function without Holl. Drearily, he unpacked, and started to repack; he was not allowed much luggage to travel with him; he would have to abandon his typewriter. But what did one wear to go to war? He went to the Mess to find out; Harold Hockey, the only person there, greeted him warmly but was not well-informed about the best dress to take to battle, beyond that he personally was not intending to take his mess kit. Alan went back; he packed normal underwear, boots, uniform, etc. He contemplated the bright blue corduroy slacks he had used for riding in, and packed them too; there seemed to be lots of room, so he packed a further four books of poetry, and a very magnificent dressing gown of silk with Chinese dragons on it, that he had bought from a peddler. Also all Lettice's letters, stuffed into the toes of his slippers. He found his squash racket standing in a corner, and made a few passes with it at the wall, but abandoned it for the Training Battalion. Then it was all done; yet he did not feel equipped.

Restless, he went down to see how his platoon was getting on; he felt able to cope with them, trained to buzz with the best of them. He found the havildar carrying out a kit inspection. Clean, smart, well-pressed and alert, his platoon was admirable; they seemed to have got on admirably too without him, and no doubt would manage somehow to get on with him too. And his havildar, a spare small man with a rich moustache, who seemed always welded into his uniform and was surely old enough to be Alan's father, greeted him with warm yet respectful pleasure; they talked together, slowly, owing to Alan's Urdu, but professionally, about the novelties revealed by the Signals Course. Alan told the havildar of the wonders of walkie-talkie wireless sets. The havildar had heard of them, but never seen one. And would they be issued shortly?

'Ultimately,' said Alan, quoting his recent instructors, 'these fine sets will be issued to every battalion in the Indian Army.' Translating 'ultimately' was difficult; the nearest he could manage in Urdu (though it was in fact very near) was 'in the end.'

'In the end,' repeated the havildar, expressionless, looking straight in front of him.

'Yes,' said Alan. Perhaps it was a phrase with which the havildar was well acquainted. 'In the end.'

'Yes,' said the havildar, and sighed, and then, catching Alan's eye, laughed.

The atmosphere in the Mess that night was subdued, vague, but a little grim. People came and went with the abstracted yet concentrated faces of men who have forgotten something vital and are on the brink of remembering what it was. Scrapings appeared for the meal, and, by order, Alan sat next to him answering a series of courteous questions about the course. Scrapings obviously was not listening to his answers. For a few moments in the middle of the meal almost all officers were present, but conversation languished between a sporadic carrying on of regimental business over the table. No one seemed more than half there.

Next day Alan's duties took him past the local Military Hospital

After a moment's hesitation, he drove his truck in. He located Holl without difficulty, directed from one flashing Eurasian grin of a nurse to the next; everyone seemed to know Holl. In a small ward he found two empty beds, and a third from which, in maroon-and-yellow-striped pyjamas, Holl protruded giant and captive, aground on his pillows. His eyes were closed, his mouth slightly open, and he was snoring with a calm rhythmical purr like a strong engine ticking over. On his right a large window was open on to the deep shade of a balcony, and beyond the parapet flat and dry and brown, India too stretched inert under the level pressure of the noon heat. With positive envy, Alan remembered how it was to lie becalmed in the hammock of a light fever, unresponsible, floating in a haze of unresolved dreams while warm sleep lapped around, and, every now and then, over. The world was quite still; even the regular purr had stopped. Half-open, but void, Holl's eyes shone at him, without recognition. Holl's skin seemed to have shrunk to a size too small, dry and yellowish; the bleak anatomy of bone and muscle threatened to slough it off at any moment. Like a corpse, his presence exhausted the surrounding air of all purpose, and Alan found himself breathing with difficulty, and his mind began to close as within the drawing of blinds. But then the eyes opened a little wider, and the pale slits flickered. Holl exclaimed aloud, and his whole body moved in a long jerk.

'Christ!' he said, rather querulous. 'I thought it was my baby brother.' He wiped his face with the sleeve of his pyjamas, looked at the sleeve, groaned, and slewed sideways in the bed for a glass of water. Refreshed, he was almost sitting up. 'You're like him,' he said, but still querulous. 'I suppose you're much the same sort. Clever boy. Not like me. Booksy, scholarships, university, the works.'

'Jimmie,' said Alan. 'We've been through this routine before. What's he up to?'

'Heh?'

'Your young brother Jimmie; what's he doing nowadays?'

'He's dead,' said Holl, and wiped his brow again. 'Flipping Frogs got him, in Syria, our gallant allies, in '40. Clever boy, he was. Hated my guts. We used to fight like cats whenever we met, which wasn't often, but he was years younger, and lighter, though crafty. He always lost; poor old Jimmie! Yes. He always lost. But a lovely tongue he had; he'd make me madder quicker than anyone I ever met. Now...' The bed suddenly shook and rattled; Holl was shaking himself like a dog. Then his eyes, fully awake and alert, looked calculatingly at Alan.

'What does that chart say?' he said, as an order.

Alan stooped at the end of the bed, and unhooked the temperature chart. It was fairly rugged. 'Hundred and one this morning, it looks like.'

'Christ! That means another three days at least. You're not on the move yet? I've never been more than six days on this bloody lark; that's three gone already. If they don't murder me with this bloody atabrin.' He was becoming more animated, with a glittering eye; he leaned sideways to Alan, and said hoarsely: 'Did you see that peach with a mole by her left eye? That's a peach. She gave me a bed-bath. A beeyoutiful, play-tonic thing. She swabbed me down as tender as a new car having its first wash, and did I stir? Not a blink. Remarkable; I knew I was pretty far gone then; she ought to try now, I said to her this morning. Caught her a flip on the passing crupper, and it did me a world of good.'

He beamed on Alan for a moment's silent reminiscence. Then he turned on his back again. 'And where have those flipping little Japs got to this morning?'

'Well, they've sunk the *Prince of Wales* and the *Repulse* off Singapore.'

Holl knew that, but he groaned. 'Poor sods. Usual stuff, it sounds like. Not a British plane in sight.'

'Penang looks as though it's about to go.'

'Ah.' Holl sucked at his teeth restlessly. 'Wish I'd listened to the geography lessons at school a bit harder. Don't suppose they've come clean, where we're going? No? Not that they need to. We're going East, my boy, and don't you believe anyone who says we aren't. One month from now, or less, we'll be in action.' The gold tooth shone brilliantly. 'Rangoon, or Singapore. Maybe for a change they'll have stopped withdrawing by the time we get there. But I'll be with you boy, you don't leave without Holl. I've got it all laid on; I'll know when you're going five minutes after you do.'

He heaved a long sigh, and closed his eyes. Then he gave Alan a series of directives: messages to his V.C.O.s and to the adjutant; he asked Alan to see that his kit was ready to go. 'And you'd better be off now. If a Sister catches you in here, there'll be blue murder. They're a sad lot, the Sisters. I have taken a vow, my boy, that if I get out of here alive, I'm going to take the Sister in charge of this lot of wards out on a bend. They just don't know, you know; there they are, withering hourly in all that starch, and all they want is a man, if only they had a clue. After all, they sacrifice themselves for us, bless 'em. 'Sonly fair we should sacrifice ourselves for them – just once, if never again.'

In spite of the vivacious wink of Holl's goodbye, Alan did not really believe that Holl would be with them when they embarked, and indeed, when the order did come through five days later, Holl was still in hospital. Alan did not have time even to get up to say goodbye to him. The departure, entraining, disentraining and embarkation at Bombay took its course with the usual chaos, high temper and boredom. A sudden lull in the turmoil, after uncounted hours, underfed and underslept, had suddenly washed Alan up on the quayside at Bombay; for a moment he stood, disorientated, purposeless. By some unexplained miracle, the battalion was almost completely embarked and settled more or less into its allotted areas aboard. The ship was not a large one, but in normal times it worked the Calcutta-Singapore route in the coolie trade, and had therefore large clear decks forward admirably adapted for what were considered to be the needs of Indian troops.

Over Alan's head, an obscure burden swung through the air towards the ship. At his side, a voice said, in the lilting Welsh of Indian English: 'That, in my humble opinion, is conclusive. We go to the Middle East, to the desert.'

It was Alan's brother officer, Second-Lieutenant Attar Singh, who was in charge of the transport, and he was pointing up at the crane; the object swinging towards the ship was a brand-new 15-cwt truck. 'Six of them were waiting here for us; all newly painted in desert camouflage. They would not issue them to us if we were going to jungle country. Let alone the fact that they have issued warm battle-dress.'

Alan hadn't thought of that, but the argument did not seem conclusive; indeed, from his own relatively limited experience of the grinding of the mills of higher command, he would have said that it was equally likely to be evidence that they were going to a bright green country. He was just about to say so when he remembered that his companion was an Indian, and, from some obscure sense of loyalty to British efficiency, restrained himself.

'But what are these?' Attar Singh was prying around on the quay; he had found some large cardboard boxes. Alan bent to look, and, shuffling one of the boxes around, discovered that they were wireless sets. He was enchanted, and delighted that he had restrained his cynicism. His belief that some power actually knew that the battalion was going somewhere (and perhaps even knew where it was going), and was brooding over its well-being with love and forethought, flickered into life again. He was just bustling off to ensure that the sets got aboard, and to dazzle his havildar with this fine new toy, when a tall figure came striding along the quay with a huge majestic gait and a flurry of agitated dock officials in its wake.

'Holl!' cried Alan, and the world lit up with the flat but breathtaking exhilaration of a flare.

Holl came to a stop. He looked very yellow; his eyes very bright. 'Nice to see you, Alan. Uh only just made it. Just brush these little bastards off me, if you would; it would be a kindness – they say Uh've no authori-tee to take part in this riot. I must find the C.O.' He snapped smartly at his besiegers, and burst up the gangplank, leaving them wailing.

Some hours later, with his men settled apparently more or less contentedly in their allotted area, Alan bumped into Holl, who was talking with one of the other company commanders.

'Of course we're going East,' he was saying. 'Any child of six could tell you. Any Japanese child of two could tell you.'

The other man was sticking to the old rumour about Ceylon. 'It stands to reason you wouldn't put in a brigade of half-trained troops into a campaign, when you had a trained brigade of some maturity standing by in a place like Ceylon which is on the way; you'd put in the older troops and replace them in Ceylon by the new ones. But anyway, Scrapings'll be back from the brigadier with the orders any moment now. Then we'll know.'

Holl had lost interest; he was whispering urgently in Alan's ear to find out where the bar was. 'Just a quick one, old boy. I'll pass out if I don't have one. Bloody bug seems to have gone to my legs.'

When Holl was sitting in the lights of what was destined to be the Officers' Mess, Alan saw that indeed he looked odd: yellower than ever, with the twitching tiredness of a very old man. Holl took two large whiskies very fast, and started back at once for his troop-decks. Outside the door, they ran into the adjutant.

'Have you seen the C.O.? That ruddy M.O. insists on saying goodbye to him personally. As if I hadn't got enough on my plate without – '

'*Goodbye*?' said Holl.

'Yes. Oh, you didn't know, I suppose. The doctor's not coming with us. He's got some special contract in his terms of service; he's strictly for within India only. No overseas nonsense for him, sensible chap. We were supposed to be having a replacement, but now we don't get one till we get to the other end.'

Holl thought, visibly as usual when assimilating some difficult problem, his fingers mashing. 'What you mean is that that bazaar-wallah is welshing on us?'

'Yes, I mean, no, not really. He's been very good, actually; he's entirely within his rights, and he needn't even have come this far.'

Holl whistled, and rocked rhythmically on his toes. 'Ah. I think I'll just have a word with Master Swami-Sawbones. He might change his mind, mightn't he?'

'Not he,' said the adjutant, but Holl had already gone.

The adjutant looked after him, slightly suspicious. 'Alan, has Sam been drinking?'

'Two whiskies. He ought to be all right.'

'Oh. Well, perhaps you might just follow him up and see he doesn't do anything stupid.'

Alan did not know where the M.O. was, and spent some minutes circling in the dark and narrow corridors of the ship. Someone told him the M.O. was in a cabin, and after some trials he found the right one.

As he opened the door, he saw, opposite him in the narrow

cubicle, the M.O. sitting on the bunk. He was a mild, spectacled man, wearing khaki slacks and tunic; his hands rested calmly on his thighs. Beside him on the bunk stood three shiny suitcases and a valise, with his mackintosh and cap on top of them. He was saying, mildly, but with a certain severe firmness: 'Now that is not an honourable suggestion for an English gentleman to make.'

All that Alan could see of Holl was his back, which was slightly hunched and marked with dark streaks of sweat, and his fists, which were enormous at the end of his slightly bent arms. He had never before noticed that Hall's hands were at least two sizes too large even for that huge body. Alan slid in sideways and shut the door. Holl's face was visible now to him, and it appalled Alan. It was swollen, and bright orange, the eyes rimmed with red, the pupils shrunken to black dots in the cold, dilated grey irises; his upper lip was set and straight, and against it the lower lip mashed up and down, emitting a stream of the foulest insults that Alan had ever heard in sequence.

'Captain Holl,' interrupted the doctor, not moving and apparently well in control; 'you are a sick man. You do not know what you are saying. I advise you very earnestly to return to your own cabin and lie down. I will give you a sedative...'

Holl took no notice; the invective proceeded, low, vibrant, and with an unrelenting flat trajectory like a high-pressure hose.

The doctor stood up. He appealed, with a trembling but half-smiling scornful dignity, to Alan: 'Mr. Mart, I fear that Captain Holl is not only sick but that he has had one go, as you say, too many at the bottle. Perhaps you could help him?' A little line of sweat shone on his upper lip, and he wiped it off with a handkerchief startlingly white against his brown skin. The gesture seemed to exasperate Holl beyond control.

'Sam!' cried Alan. It was the first time he had called Holl by his Christian name, and afterwards he remembered this.

'You get to hell out of here. This doctor's coming with us if I have to knock him cold and lock him up until we've sailed.'

As Holl took one step forward, his fists coming up, a curious movement, as formal and detached as a ballet sequence, involved the three men, and Alan saw it happening as though he himself were only a spectator of it. The Indian, with an easy and graceful gesture, put one hand on the steel wall of the cabin as if to steady himself and with the other hand took off his spectacles; simultaneously, Alan turned inwards to restrain Holl. Holl handed him off with all his strength, yet caught him by the shirt collar as he did so, so that as Alan fell backwards he was checked, and then heaved up on the reflex against Holl's body, jolted loose as a rag doll. On the fall backwards, his right hand flung out behind him to break the fall; on the rebound, as Holl heaved him up again, his arm came swinging forward out of control in a swinging arc, and met the Indian's cheek in a loose, very loud flat smack, just as the door behind him opened, and their commanding officer stood among them. The movement froze. Alan lay off-balance across Holl's chest, and the Indian stood bent over, leaning on the hand that held his spectacles on the bunk, with the other hand to his cheek, and an expression of pure astonishment in his eyes. Scrapings stood there between them now, almost as tall as Holl, gaunt, his heavy moustache hiding his mouth, his dark eyes blank under the furious clench of his thick eyebrows.

The cabin was so small that all the men were almost touching; from his inclined position, Alan found that he was looking up Scrapings' nostrils which were armoured with crisp grey hairs. A low panting noise was going on, but beneath that there was a silence opening like a void between a man fallen overboard and his ship.

Into this gap at last Scrapings' voice moved. 'Well?' he said, with a hopeless fluttering motion of his hands.

Tears had started to run down the Indian's cheeks; he muttered something unintelligible.

Scrapings inhaled, looking round the group, his head moving stiffly like a gun-turret. Then his eyebrows came down, and he roared at Alan: 'Stand *up*!'

Alan righted himself, lurching. The collar of his shirt was torn, and flapped loosely, exposing his collarbone; with one hand, he scrabbled at it.

The Indian had found words now, and was voluble. 'Sir, these men have assaulted me! Disgracefully they came to insult me; having insulted me to their filthy satisfaction, they have assaulted me.' He waved a hand. 'See. They have broken my spectacles! Although prudently I removed them, suspecting.' He held them up; he must have half-fallen on them, and one side-piece was missing. The tears rolled faster down his face; his voice became piteous, imploring. 'Sir! I ask justice. I have only done my best, always put my best foot forward. Only to be now insulted, beaten up by these hooligans. Sir – '

'Holl! Mart! You will return to your quarters and stay there until you hear from me.'

'But, *sir* – ' Alan began.

'Get *out*!'

In the corridor, Holl stood still. He shook his head as though a fly were worrying it. He shook it again. Then, without a glance at Alan, he went off towards his cabin supporting himself every now and then with one hand against the wall.

In his own minute cabin, Alan mechanically removed his torn shirt, and got out another one. Then he washed thoroughly in the little folding basin: his hands seemed to reek with an odour like that of crushed nettles. Then he put on his clean shirt and sat on his bunk, his hands dangling, his eyes shut, trying not to remember the doctor's face of outrage, and trying to banish the thought that this must be the end of Holl. After an interminable time, an orderly knocked at his door, and Alan followed him to the cabin that the C. O. had taken as his office. Holl was already there, standing stiffly to attention; Alan joined him, and they stood looking over the top of Scrapings' head as he fiddled with a pencil at his desk. The door shut.

'Now,' said the C.O., 'this is a miserable business.' His eyes remained miserably on his pencil, and Alan saw, for the first time, that he was going bald on the top of his head, with some thin grey hairs dispersed inadequately over a sheen of vulnerable skin. 'The M.O.'s story is that Holl came to his cabin, was drunk, and started to insult him; he was joined by you, Mart, and you both insulted him and then assaulted him, breaking his spectacles. What have you to say to that?' He looked up at them; he was obviously very tired.

'Well, sir...' said Alan and Holl together.

'Holl, first.'

'Well, sir, that's all perfectly true. Up to a point. I understood from the adjutant that the M.O. was ratting on us, sir – '

'That is not correct. He was perfectly within his legal rights.'

Holl leaned forward with a bright flush, and an emphatic forefinger. 'Ah, sir, but his *moral* rights? What about – '

'I'm not asking for an apologia, Holl. I want to know what happened.' For the first time his voice had an edge to it.

Holl recoiled to attention. 'Sir. I thought it to be my duty to attempt to dissuade the M.O. from leaving the ship. So I called on him, sir, and tried to reason with him, quite calmly, sir, to try – '

Alan suppressed a gasp.

'To make him understand that a man with any guts, let alone any conscience just could *not* – '

'Holl! I want to know what *happened*.'

'I was arguing with him, sir, when Alan here came in. And Alan must have mistaken something I said, and have thought, sir, that I was going to hit the little ba – I mean, sir, he seems to have tried to stop me. Then I'm afraid I lost my temper, and quite inadvertently hit the swine – I mean the M.O. – with Alan. It was entirely accidental, sir.'

Scrapings put his head between his hands, and groaned aloud. Then he looked up again. 'Had you been drinking?'

'Only two whiskies.' He appealed to Alan for confirmation.

'Yes, sir. Only two whiskies.'

The C.O. looked helplessly round the cabin, and then back to Holl. 'You were properly discharged from hospital this morning?'

After a perceptible pause, Holl launched his lie as gracefully as a clay pigeon. 'Yes, sir. They all thought I'd made a remarkable recovery.'

Alan thought Scrapings must burst now, but instead he put his head into his hands again; then he looked up.

'Have you anything to add to that, Mart?'

'No, sir.'

'But it was you who hit the M.O.?'

Holl interrupted. 'No, sir. It was I; I hit the M.O. with Alan.'

Without warning, Scrapings blew up. 'Hold your bloody tongue!' For a few moments he simply shouted at them, as his face warmed from grey to a very reddish purple. His voice cracked, and he had to pause for breath. Taking almost visible grip on his rage, he summed up, still shouting, but on a low register. They had disgraced themselves – the battalion – the Indian Army – the whole service. They had committed a grave offence; of its gravity not only was he, Scrapings, well aware, but he had reason to think that the M.O. was equally well aware of its gravity. The M.O. had demanded a court-martial, and a court-martial there would certainly have to be, with ensuing repercussions, not merely local – the politicians would certainly get hold of it. At this thought, the tirade ceased; Scrapings' head rocked to and fro with the horror of it, his eyes shut. Then he said, quietly, that they were to consider themselves under open arrest and to withdraw to their cabins; he would have to think out whether they could sail with the boat or not.

Here Holl broke in; standing like a bound prisoner, his head straining forward on its neck, he said: 'Sir, I must insist that Alan had nothing to do with this.'

'Hold your tongue!'

'Also,' continued Holl, drawing his head back, and his voice suddenly mild as milk and almost coy; 'with the deepest respect, sir, but if you mean to get me off this boat before it sails you'll have to have me carried off in chains.'

Scrapings jerked violently, and the purple in his cheeks began to mantle again. He gasped, but havered, so taken aback, and his moustache, as if endowed with a life of its own, twitched and bristled along the line of his mouth. He lowered his head again so that they could not see his face.

'That's enough, Holl.' He was looking at his watch. 'You will return to your quarters, but before you do so, there is one thing that must be done. The M.O. will be leaving the ship at any moment, and you will apologise to him before he goes. I shall have to thrash out this wretched business later.'

Holl started forward again, his eyes popping. '*Apologise*!' He was profoundly shocked.

'Apologise,' agreed Scrapings, hard and level. 'It's about your only hope, apart from any other considerations. I don't suppose for a moment that it'll have the least effect. But you will, by God, apologise forthwith. That is an order.'

Dumbfounded, Holl looked at him. Then he saluted.

'Mart,' said Scrapings. 'You wait one moment.'

The door shut behind Holl. Scrapings was now looking round and over Alan with an expression of concentrated but incredulous distaste. Then he said, in a ringing, raging but baffled shout: 'When I was a younger man – !' He stopped.

He proceeded, his voice mild now as Holl's had been, with also an almost wistful undertone. 'Perhaps there is no more honour left. I *saw* you slap that wretched Indian, with my own eyes I saw you, so help me God. Has it not occurred to you, you filthy little puppy, that to take advantage of another man's weakness – a brother-officer's sickness – that to shield behind his... his...' Scrapings' voice wavered, and sunk even softer. His purple had faded to an ashen-grey. He found the word. 'To take advantage of his *generosity...*' His voice faded altogether.

Alan stood with his mouth open, but speechless. The blood roared in his head.

'Well?' said Scrapings after a time. 'Have you nothing to say for yourself?'

Alan's mouth shut with an audible snap. 'No,' he said.

Scrapings' eyes roved in contempt over him. 'In that case you'd better get after your victim fast, and apologise. Having done that you will return to your quarters and not budge until you are told.'

Alan turned to go.

A roar halted him. Scrapings was standing now behind his desk, an enraged trembling hand flung out towards Alan. 'By God, don't you ever condescend to *salute* your senior officers, you guttersnipe? *Salute*, damn you!'

Alan turned, shaking, and saluted rigidly.

'Get out,' observed Scrapings, baring his teeth, and turned his back on him.

Alan fled down the narrow steel passageways, bumping off bulwarks and people indiscriminately. The cabin where they had interviewed the doctor was empty. Alan stumbled on up a companionway on to the shrouded darkness of the deck. He sighted the M.O. just turning on to the gangway down to the quayside. He caught him by the sleeve.

The doctor half-turned, and shook Alan's hand indignantly from his sleeve as if it were unclean. 'First one and now the other,' he moaned, and then, hissing: 'Don't touch me! Go away. I do not wish to speak to you, Jao!' he added urgently to the two orderlies who were preceeding him down the gangway with his bags. 'Go! Go quickly!'

'I want to apologise,' said Alan, fawning. 'To apologise.'

The doctor was stumbling away down the gangplank, one hand holding the broken spectacles on to his nose, the other making a fanning movement before his face like a publicity-shy celebrity. 'Go away!' he was repeating shrilly. 'Go away! I do not hear.' By the time he reached the quay he was running, almost reeling, out of sight into the darkness.

Alan clung to the salt-damp stanchion at the top of the gangway, motionless. Then he lifted both fists, as though to beat at something. His hands dropped open and empty to his sides. 'I'm sorry,' he said, softly. 'I'm sorry.'

He seemed to have been sitting in his cabin forever. It was a tiny compartment, closed and self-sufficient as a cell, and stiflingly hot. Over the porthole, which he could not open, hung a diminutive curtain of an incongruous chintz. He sat on the narrow bunk, as the doctor had sat, ready to go, with his valise and his suitcase beside him, and on top of them his raincoat, hat and stick.

He had two callers at his door. The first knock had been Sundar Singh's, a timid, stuttering rap. Alan had told him to go away, without rising or opening the door. The second knock had been firmer, and he had risen from the bunk with no doubt at all that this was the escort to take him ashore, when he heard Holl's voice, whispering raucously outside.

'Go away,' said Alan, to the locked door, and kept on saying it, tired but stubborn as the doctor, until Holl had gone away, swearing but unadmitted. The world seemed full of backs withdrawing into the night, saying: *Go away*. All round him, echoing the length and breadth of the ship, men moved restlessly to and fro, scurrying like rats' feet. At last through the muted turmoil instead of the escort's summons at his door, there came a grinding clanking clamour, with shouts and knocking thuds. The ship shuddered, and a few moments later he realised that it was moving. He did not understand, and sat, still waiting for something else to happen. By his watch, it was 3a.m. He had had almost nothing to eat for over twenty-four hours. Presently the little chintz curtain began to swing in and out from its rail; the quiver of the ship settled to a steadier throb. They must be at sea. He was under way, under close arrest, to an undivulged destination.

Sometime after this, Holl's voice sounded again outside his door, louder now and more confident, stating that if Alan did not let him in he would break the door down. Immediately, in earnest of this, the door shook before a massive onslaught. Drearily, Alan rose to open it.

Holl came in. He was excited; his eyes overbright, and very high in colour. 'We're clear,' he said. 'I knew old Scrapings wouldn't sail without me.' He stood there looking at Alan, who had relapsed on to his bunk again. Holl cleared his throat. 'Without us,' he amended. 'What d'you think?'

Alan looked up at him and thought. With careful deliberation, he said: 'I think you are the most contemptible swine I've ever had the bad luck to do with. I think you should be handed over bound hand and foot to that wretched little doctor so that he could flog the skin off you with a dog whip. I think – '

Holl, his eyes popping, put out a hand, patting him down, soothing, as though Alan were deranged. 'Now look, sonny.' He stopped, and waved Alan over on the bunk to make room for him. 'Move over so's I can sit down.' Alan snarled at him.

'*Move*!' said Holl, with explosive force, and, automatically, Alan moved.

'That's better,' said Holl. 'I'm *tired*!'

They sat in a row: Holl, Alan, a valise and a suitcase. Holl sighed, turned to Alan, and laid a hand on his knee which jerked away as if stung. 'For God's sake!' cried Holl. 'Anyone'd think you were on *his* side. Now look, sonny; let's be reasonable. We don't want to get all emotional and het-up, do we? All right – the little man had his contract with the government, and he was only to serve in India. All right – though if I hear that word, con-*truct*, again I shall scream. But what about his con-truct with getting on for a thousand bodies of flesh and blood in his care? What about that? If you were him, would you walk out on a battalion of men going into action and leave them without a doctor?'

'To begin with,' said Alan, 'you are setting up as judge of another man's conscience. And by what right? Then this doctor is also an Indian. He has no contract legal or moral with the Army beyond the terms he freely agreed to and which the Army freely agreed to. You're just the sort of bloody sentimentalist and flag-wagging thug that's going to wreck the noble dissolution of a fine empire before we've even saved it from the Japs to dissolve. This man is a mercenary; he's committed by no ties, not one damn' tie in the world, to your or my snivelling, selfish patriotism. You're a press gang, Holl; I thought we stopped using them two hundred years ago, but here you still are beating up and then morally blackmailing that decent little rabbit. For Christ's sake, did you not see his face! Anyone'd think your hobby was daily rape.'

Holl looked rather dazed. Groping, he began again: 'Now, *look*, sonny...' and again Alan's knee avoided his hand. Heatedly, Holl said: 'But he's an *Indian*! And ninety-nine per cent of the battalion are his brown-skinned brothers, and you're saying, if I follow you, that he owes no duty to them?' His voice tailed off; he looked wildly bewildered, and then another thought struck him. 'Alan,' he said, 'you can't *say* things like that – those are dirty thoughts; for God's sake, it's sheer defeatism – '

At that moment the door opened, and the adjutant appeared. He came in, and shut the door behind him with his foot. He was carrying two plates of curry and chapatti.

'All the criminals sharing the same cell?' His jocularity rang like a cracked and tired bell. 'I thought maybe you were hungry; I discovered suddenly I was ravenous myself. Well, Scrapings has taken a risk on you both; maybe you'll be ordered back straightaway on the next boat; maybe not. Depends on how much stink our medical friend raises with his friends in India. And on where we turn out to be going to. Scrapings has a sealed envelope that he's got to open tomorrow and then we shall all know.'

'No need to worry about that,' said Holl. 'Where we're going they will want any able bodies too much to spare them for the luxury of a court-martial.'

The adjutant was saying his bet was Basra, but Holl went on: 'I'd like to apologise to you for all this blithering fuss. I feel,' he said generously, with a wide gesture, 'that in a way it's all my fault, though with the best of intentions – '

'Skip it,' said the adjutant. 'Spilt milk, and so on. What I want to know is just what happened; Scrapings has a very weird version, and I felt he must have got something wrong somewhere.'

Holl told him.

When he had done, the adjutant turned in bewilderment to Alan. 'What in hell's name did *you* tell Scrapings? According to him, you were at the bottom of the whole thing, and you hit the man.'

'What!' Holl was indignant. 'But I told him.'

'It seems,' said Alan, wearily, 'that I hit the man, and that now I am shielding, Holl, behind your generosity, thank you, Holl, who is nobly trying to take the blame. But our clear-eyed C.O. saw through your bluff, Holl, because his clear eyes saw my hand hit the poor wretch. I take it that Scrapings thinks you were trying to stop me bashing the M.O. about. You know what I am.' He was getting a little hysterical.

'Oh, Jesus,' said Holl. 'I don't understand; say it all over again slowly. And shut that door; there's the hell of a draught.' He wiped his forearm across his forehead, and blinked, and prepared to concentrate on Alan again. But Alan and the adjutant had glanced at the door. The door was shut, and glancing back at Holl, they both recognised at once the fever brilliant in his eyes and burning in cold sweat on his face.

'Shut it!' said Holl. 'And get a move on, Alan.' He swayed backwards, and righted himself with an effort, looking angrily round.

The adjutant and Alan looked at each other. 'You'd better run and find the ship's doctor,' said the adjutant.

A few minutes later, under the irate and sleepy eye of the ship's doctor, they were supporting gingerly an almost unconscious Holl along the passages towards the sick bay, where they left him.

'*Christ*!' said the adjutant. 'What a send-off! Wish us good luck as you wave us goodbye.' He looked closely at Alan. 'Don't worry, Alan, it'll all come out in the wash. I'll prise the truth into Scrapings somehow, though I'd keep as clear of him as you can manage for the moment, if I were you. You'd better try and get a couple of hours' sleep.'

Outside Alan's door they paused. The responsibility of the administration of the battalion seemed to come down on the adjutant like a sudden weight. He muttered confusedly about seeing to this and seeing to that, swaying on his feet, almost asleep as he talked. Coming to for a moment, he looked in puzzled and distressed accusation at Alan. 'All the same,' he said, 'you might have taken a bit better care of him; he's a sick man, you know.'

He turned on his heel, and wavered off to his office.

Alan had shut himself in his room before he realised that Sundar Singh was already in there too. In the brief interval that Alan had been out the orderly had managed to get most of his master's belongings out of their travelling cases, but not to dispose of them anywhere.

Alan groaned, and told the boy to go away; to go to bed.

'But, sahib...'

Alan repeated his request, but the boy still bumbled about the little room. Alan said the confusion could keep till the morning. But still Sundar Singh did not go; he seized in triumph a pair of Alan's boots, holding them aloft. Could he clean them?

'Yes, of course. But go; it is after four o'clock. *Sleep*.'

The boy hung on at the door, still reluctant.

'What is it?'

'Sahib, sahib, that doctor sahib is a *badmash*; no good.'

In the' midst of his weariness, Alan was so surprised by this that he sat down on his bunk with a jerk. The orderly's round face looked at him with serious wonder.

'No,' said Alan. 'You must not say that for it is not true. The doctor has done nothing wrong; he has done his duty.' Sickly, he realised that the whole ship must know already – but how much did they know, what version did they know? And above all, what did they feel about it? He dared not ask.

'*Ram ram*,' he said. 'Thank you; now get along and sleep.'

'*Ram ram*, sahib.' The orderly's departing grin lingered like a flickering buoy-light in the sweating, sleepless nightmare, throbbing in time with the ship's engines, into which Alan gradually lowered himself in his bunk.

The next morning, all officers were summoned to conference by the C.O. at eight o'clock. Alan, slinking along the ship's corridors, was the last to arrive. Everyone was there except Holl.

'Gentlemen,' said the C.O., 'I have just opened the orders handed to me by the brigadier yesterday.' He paused. Alan glowed towards him with a steady hatred.

'Our destination, gentlemen, is Malaya.' The assembled officers swayed slightly, but made no sound. 'We should disembark, in ten days' to a fortnight's time, at Singapore. Every effort will be made (I quote) to afford the brigade time to acclimatise, but each unit must be fully prepared to go into action against the enemy upon embarkation if necessary.'

Somebody deflated with an audible phew.

Scrapings tossed the paper on to the table, and looked round the company. 'Now that is all I know. I need not remind you that is neither what we hoped for nor what we have been trained for, but in war few things turn out as one expects. I have every confidence in you and in the men that I am fortunate enough to command: that you will bear yourselves in accordance with the traditions of this regiment and of the Indian Army. We may be young troops, but if so, the better perhaps our wind and the fresher our courage. Now, I have a few general points to make. Firstly, morale. It is vital on a voyage in cramped quarters like this, and particularly a little later when we shall certainly have to face the threat of air attack, to keep the men busy and cheerful...'

Grudgingly, Alan thought that the old man was putting it

across with remarkable dignity. Composedly, with due gravity and decorum, the voice continued. Now, Scrapings was indicating with a pencil a large atlas propped open on a sideboard. 'There is Malaya.'

The pendulous peninsula, painted red for Britain, drooped from Asia into the scattered islands of the East Indies. Alan thought that it looked like a large blood-stained cosh.

'According to this morning's news, the enemy are...' The outlandish names clanged like tin-pot gongs – Kelantan, Taiping, Grik – and then were absorbed into the familiar jargon of bulletins: '...driven off with heavy casualties to the enemy.' Then, ominously overfamiliar: 'British forces south of Kedah were successfully disengaged during the night.'

Scrapings cleared his throat, and summed up. 'The British line seems therefore to be held from east to west some – hum – some fifty to seventy miles from the southernmost part of the Thailand frontier.' He peered at the map.

'How far is that from Singapore?' said a voice.

Scrapings fixed his eyes on the ceiling, and frowned.

The voice rephrased the question. 'I mean, sir, what is the size of this country?'

Scrapings glanced at his notes. 'About 450 miles from north to south.'

Alan thought that sounded quite a long way; he had had an uncomfortable notion it was only about 200 miles.

Scrapings was going on. 'Elsewhere the Japanese appear to have made successful – *momentarily* successful – landings in North Borneo' – the pencil swooped over the map – 'and – in Sarawak.' The pencil looped about the south of Malaya, and Alan wondered, hollowly, what resistance there was in Borneo, Sarawak, Java, Sumatra, to stop the completion of that arc into the encirclement of Malaya.

Scrapings said that they now knew as much as he did, but that he was open to questions, before proceeding to routine matters.

'The country; sir – I take it that it's fairly heavily wooded?'

Scrapings grinned; it looked more like a snarl. 'I believe you take it correctly. Rubber plantations; palm; swamp; jungle; rivers. I'm afraid our desert training will be somewhat supernumerary; we may, however, have the consolation that doubtless when we have knocked the Japanese out of the jungle, we shall then be sent as jungle experts to the Sahara.'

At this simple joke, the uneasy tension in the crowded room broke. Suddenly united in confidence, the officers nudged each other, and laughed. Smiling, Alan too turned warmly to share the joke with his neighbour. He found that he was standing next to the Sikh transport officer, and smiled on him. The Indian's face closed; his nostrils dilated slightly, and under the silken moustaches his mouth curled. With a faint *pfui* of disgust, he stood away from Alan.

Red-faced, Alan stood alone in the joking and now loquacious crowd. Scrapings was moving about amongst them, talking almost lightheartedly. He came up to the Sikh. 'I want you,' he said, 'to take over D Company for the time being. Captain Holl, as you know, is sick, though he will be back in the near future. In the meantime...'

The Sikh stood rigidly to attention; his eyes shone mildly, with gratified self-confidence and authority. All the officers suddenly hushed, and they glanced briefly sideways, not at the Sikh, but at Alan, before resuming their conversation.

After disposing of routine daily orders, Scrapings announced adjournment until after breakfast. The officers cleared from the room so that the stewards might prepare for the meal. Hockey was the last of them out. 'How anyone could be crass enough,' he was saying, 'to let poor old Sam within a mile of a whisky bottle. I mean there he was, I don't suppose he'd eaten a crumb all day and with a temperature of 104; why even one small peg would bowl anyone over in that state.'

Alan found that he was alone in the room.

With slow deliberation, the little convoy, shepherded by bounding frigates, pushed southwards in the bright blue sea. At frequent, irregular intervals each ship seethed with boat drills and A.R.P. exercises. Unwontedly large and rich meals came and went in the Officers' Mess. Alan busied himself with his new wireless sets; after abandoning the attempt to initiate his platoon in the theory of wireless communication (for his Urdu could not grapple even with elementary phrases such as 'wave length'), he devised a drill. Soon his men were sitting about crooning the formulae of communication, assembling the sets, running up aerials, clicking switches, adjusting knobs and watching dials with a reverence all the more profound because the magic boxes remained forever silent. Alan had been forbidden to send any live signals in case they should reveal the convoy's position to enemy forces.

Christmas Day came, weirdly stifling. The weather had congealed into a hot humidity; moving about, even on deck at night, produced a strong impression that the body was clad in damp woollen combinations. With the sweat lolling in open pores, the officers ate turkey and Christmas pudding, and wondered where they would spend next Christmas, and spoke, meandering, a little feverish, of past Christmases of peace.

That evening Alan went up on deck in the hot clinging dark that smelled of oil and salt. Forward, he found one of the ship's officers leaning over the rail; as a great favour he was asked into the wireless cabin to hear the news. So he heard that Hong Kong had fallen.

'Why the hell they ever tried to hold it is past belief,' said the ship's officer.

Then they heard, crackling, fading and surging through the thick air, the voice of the King as he gave his Christmas message. 'Be strong and of good courage,' said the King. 'Go forward into this coming year with a good heart.'

The ship's officer said that he thought the old boy's stammer was hardly noticeable now, didn't Alan agree?

Churchill was in Washington.

The ship's officer, personally, was not at all sure that the risk in ferrying Winnie to and fro across the Atlantic was worth it, just for a lot of gup with the Yanks. Alan had no views on this.

The wireless officer switched off. 'Well,' said Alan's friend, 'there we all are. There we all are. And a very happy Boxing Day to you all.' He had a thin, wedge-shaped face like a cut of Cheddar cheese. 'Still, we might be in Hong Kong. Being raped, I dare say. Got to count your blessings. And I dare say I'm better off, in this stinking old kettle, than you're likely to be a fortnight from now. I would, however, take it as a personal favour if you would refrain from staging another Dunkirk. I done that job. Let's have some air.'

They went, for a change, to the stern. It transpired that the sailor had been sunk three times already.

'Go on,' said Alan. 'You're showing off.'

'Fact. But a man gets nervous.' They watched the phosphorescent oily swag and swirl of their wake floating out behind them; on each side, almost invisible, the vague shapes of the convoy slid in silent concord with them as if drawn by wires across the flat sea. The sailor spoke with relish of his sinkings. The North Atlantic one was the worst he said: cold; bitter. '

After a time, Alan though he would go below.

'That schemozzle before we left Bombay,' said the officer. 'Funny business. Never have guessed you were the battling type; couldn't really make it all out myself, but I dare say you had your reasons?'

'Yes.'

'Oh well, don't we all? Good night.'

'Good night.'

Stretched in his bunk, Alan lay flat on his back. The narrow bunk in the narrow room was like an open iron coffin, though wadded in an open iron crypt. He lay with his hands tucked underneath him; they had developed recently, if left to themselves, a habit of spidering all over the place. He thought carefully of his home, but the iron coffin, though wadded, refused transformation into a cradle or even into the narrow iron bed in the attic where he had slept as a boy, with the sheepdog Irma across the door; and, however careful he was, he ended up by finding himself confronted by his parents; there they were listening to his explanation of the truth behind the court-martial; he had, he was saying, been unjustly cashiered, and yes, darling, of course, they said, looking at him with eyes like Irma's, full of loving condemnatory forgiveness. He turned on his face, and thought, instead, resolutely of Lettice.

He escaped with her; they were in a punt, slithering up the dark odorous river. She would lie with her face to the stars, shadowy, her feet pointing towards him as he stood, the boatman, stooping on the thrust, erect to lance the pole down, and stooping to thrust again.

'Lettice' he would say into the magic dark, as he almost walked the waters, 'Lettice. Who am I? Who are you?'

She would conjure names up to the sky, decorating the stars with labels. Belshazzar; Alcibiades; Anthony; Faust; Lucifer; Rimbaud; Harpo; Errol Flynn.

'No, no. I'm not an ambitious man. Who are you?'

'Lettice.'

'Who am I?'

'Alan Al-*lun*.' The way she spoke his name, the last syllable was perfect and final; it nailed his identity and established it like a butterfly within a showcase for eternity. With her voice alone she could so shape him, that the rider to the definition that later they would have to grope towards, with mouth on mouth, searching hands, body upon body, seemed always incomplete by comparison.

Hopefully now, lustfully almost, he listened for his name as she would say it. He mouthed it into the pillow and the pillow stifled it. He turned on his back and said her name. Lettice. It was ridiculous. Salad; a dish. His hands escaped, and one crept up the ship's wall at the side of his bunk, finding rivets there like boils; the other hand trailed, groping over the edge of the bunk. He could not even remember her shape. There remained the ache that did not know what it ached for, beyond a large blonde shape; her eyes again refused his memory.

His terror roused him to sit up, groaning. She had not answered his letter. The reasons why she had not answered fought a tired battle against his fear in the hot dark; when they had died down, there remained only the hot dark, and the perpetual throb of the ship's engines again insistent. He lay back again, void, as sweat ran from his body; he seemed to be evaporating, as a jellyfish evaporates on sun-cooked rock; to leave presently only a shadow, a stain, for the next tide to cover.

Grimly, he rallied to think again. He sat up and switched his light on; when the dazzle had subsided, his eyes rested on the clothes he had taken off: shirt, shorts, stockings, shoes. They lay confused on the floor, yet here and there, moulded or crinkled, they remembered his shape. A small relief stirred in him, and he was distracted by the dreamy thought of the ship about him moving through the ocean, littered with anonymous bodies, yet each body with its husk beside it. He thought of them; the troops on the hot decks, packed, poleaxed in that prostrate Indian sleep; the ship's crew, the captain, his brother officers, Holl in the sick bay. Then, vividly, he saw Holl as he had seen him in hospital before they sailed: bursting out of his skin, the small head almost the same width as the huge muscular neck.

Alan was out of his bunk, fuddling in a muddled way with his clothes. He hadn't been to see Holl once while he was in the sick bay. Everyone else had paid a visit. Holl was of course quite all right; the relapse had proved only momentary, and the sole reason that he was still confined within the sick bay was because Scrapings had persuaded the ship's captain, and the ship's doctor, that it would be politic for all concerned if Holl were kept in bed for the time being. But Holl would be upset that Alan hadn't come to see him.

Alan stopped fumbling with his clothes, and slowly took them off again. 'I'm going mad,' he said aloud. 'The bastard,' he said, peevish, and fell backwards into his bunk and a profound sleep.

In fact, Holl did not appear for another three days. Then, returning exasperated from a long session with his signallers and the silent wireless sets, towards lunch, Alan heard a familiar high roaring along the deck. Thoughtfully he changed direction, and withdrew to his cabin. He fed at noon, and again in the evening, from curry provided by Sundar Singh from the troops' galley, and managed, in spite of two action station exercises, to avoid Holl. But it could not last very long.

He went to bed early, so that Holl, bursting into his cabin, caught him with his trousers down. Alan became involved in an enraged and complex dance with his pyjama trousers, while Holl watched, swearing that it was good to see him again. At length, from a position of slightly less weakness, his pyjama trousers firmly knotted, Alan found voice, and suggested that Holl might leave.

Holl looked hurt. He picked Alan's clothes off the stool and dropped them on the floor and sat on the stool. He looked very fit; richly robust, and of quite good colour. He had done something to his hair, which was smoothed thinly and lustrously across the narrow skull under grease.

'You never came to see me, lad,' he said, his face sorrowfully perplexed. 'That wasn't good. That wasn't *nice*.'

'Go away.'

Holl looked him over scrupulously, still frowning. 'You're not looking well. You're worrying; I was afraid you'd be worrying. I got worrying myself lying in that antiseptic bin thinking of you worrying; you ought to have come and seen me. You're not used to these things, like I am. They just slip off; water off a duck's back.'

'What the hell have you done to your hair?' The question was wrung reluctantly, in spite of himself, from Alan. 'Oh, skip it. Just go.'

Holl blushed, and ran his hand over his head, avoiding actual contact. 'I got dandruff,' he said, shameful. 'One of the matelots passed me some brilliantine, to help it.' He was embarrassed as if he had been found guilty of some major uncleanness. He shook his head as if to dislodge it; he shook it again. Then he frowned earnestly on Alan.

'I've been thinking about you, as I said. They all seem to think it was you that hit that rat. Now, I don't like that. I hit him, and if you hadn't got in the bloody way, I'd have knocked him so cold he'd still be out. And I'd do it again. But that's not the point.' He lowered forward, breathing heavily and giving off a thick cloud of concern. 'Have they been getting at you in the Mess? By God, if they've been – been bullying you, I'll lay them out one by one. I'm not standing for it.'

'Thank you, nurse.'

'What d'you say?'

'*Nurse*. Nanny. Perambulator in starched cuffs. Perambulate off!'

Holl brushed this aside with a large meat-coloured hand, and settled his haunches more squarely on the stool. 'Have they been getting at you; that's all I want to know.'

'No. For God's sake, *no*! They've all been very gracious.' After the first day, indeed, so they had, if with a somewhat self-conscious expansiveness, making a rather larger place for him in the conversation than was necessary. Every now and then their faces would close in the high blank incomprehension of an established society into whose midst an uninvited stranger had strayed with unerring clodhopping *faux pas* and clad in outrageous clothes. But they had been very correct; he on the other hand probably tried to keep himself to himself too much.

'Of course,' he said, more to himself than to Holl, 'Attar Singh won't speak to me.'

Holl laughed. 'The poor lad had to hand my company back to me today. He wouldn't look at me. He's a grand lad. There's a fighter! If that medical baby had had a tenth of old Attar's guts, he'd be with us yet.'

Holl now relaxed, sticking one leg out in front of him, his hands on his hips. 'Well then, that's all right. I had a session with Scrapings today, and told him he'd got the wrong angle on things. He tried to shout me down, of course, but I sorted him out all right. He's all right. And I don't want you to worry, Alan, about this court-martial business: that's all my eye and Aunt Fanny. In a few days when we get off this boat, no one's going to have *time* to worry about a court-martial. They've got other business. *Our* business.'

He hitched the stool confidentially closer to the bunk. 'Now. These Japs. You know where they've got to? Not much short of 200 miles they've got inside three weeks. That's not bad. Looks to me as if we've got the most ivory-headed set of brass at the top in Singapore we've had yet, which is saying something, but even granted that, these little yellow Japanese men certainly are moving.' He paused; he shook his head with the dislodging movement; he reached forward, and tapped Alan's knees with a firm forefinger. 'We'll stop that. By God, I won't have utt!' he pronounced with massive conviction, and took over the conduct of the Malayan campaign into his own hands. He dealt sorrowfully with irrevocably past strategic decisions; he dealt with the present strategic situation; he dealt with tactical aspects of jungle warfare. With some reluctance, he conceded the possibility of the Japanese overrunning the whole country by sheer force of numbers, only to withdraw himself in lone triumph, at the head of a compact, self-sufficient guerrilla force, into the jungle. It could go on forever, he said. Singapore itself would never fall, and thence the striking forces in the jungle could be supplied by air.

Alan thought he had got far enough. 'Where's Scrapings?'

'Heh?'

'Where's Scrapings? You've taken over the battalion; not to mention the division, or the Army. You Tamburlaine.'

'Oh, Scrapings'll be all right. And if only those boys can hold where they are a couple of months, I'll have knocked this battalion into such a collection of murderous Tarzans as the world has never seen.' His face clouded. 'But the sooner we're off this boat the better. They're getting soft, the troops. Even softer than they were. As they are now, God knows what they'd do to the enemy, but by God, they frighten me.'

'Wellington.'

'What?'

'That's what Wellington said about his troops.'

'Did he now? *Did* he? Well, I'm damned.' Holl looked very pleased. 'Just goes to show. So Wellington said that, the old buzzard! And just look what he did to old Boney with those troops!'

Delighted, Holl departed, to 'get his head down.' 'Cheer up, laddie. We'll be off this boat in a couple of days and all feel better.' He brooded for a moment in the doorway. 'It's getting good and *personal*,' he said.

Alan sat for a little after Holl had gone, cracking his fingers. They cracked well and cheerfully. He got into bed, and went to sleep.

FOUR

NEXT DAY a long dark bluish green-grey edge lifted on the horizon on the east: the coast of Java. Turning northwards, the convoy crept along it. Aboard ship, the tension grew; A.R.P. exercises intensified, but the sky sweltered grey and unbroken over them. Next day they passed through the straits between Java and Sumatra, and for the first time they saw aeroplanes. Out of the east they came, marked with reassuring red, white and blue markings, sturdy, flying low with an oddly old-fashioned fussiness.

'Christ!' said Alan's friend, the ship's officer. '*Buffaloes*! Would you believe it! I thought they'd all been put painlessly to sleep years ago. Why, they can fly all of a hundred miles an hour if pushed. Let us cross our fingers, and pray.'

But they saw no Japanese planes, and they reached Singapore unmolested, at night and in heavy rain; in the dark wet, the docks might have been anywhere in the world, nor was there much sign of air raid damage about. Orderly and subdued, the battalion disembarked, and entrained immediately for a destination as usual unrevealed.

As Alan stood by his carriage door, waiting for the train to leave with all his men satisfactorily disposed, a woman in a light mackintosh came up to him, bearing gifts. It was an odd shock to see a European woman, a civilian, there. Gratefully he accepted a packet of cigarettes, but it made him uneasy to think of women and presumably children still living in Singapore. She was shouting something up to him against the escaping roar of steam; her face was turned upwards, shining pale and wet, with something touchingly forlorn and mysterious in the dark; a strand of hair strayed on her temples from under the hood of her coat.

'What?' he shouted, stooping to her.

'Thank God you've come,' she shouted. Her breath came up to him, saturated with gin as the air was with rain.

'Oh,' he said.

The train moved out. It went slowly, hesitantly, stopping

frequently, sometimes for air raid alarms, sometimes just stopping. Towards dawn Alan fell asleep, to awake apparently the next moment with a jerk. The train was stationary, and for the moment of waking he was convinced it had been ambushed; it stood in a deep narrow cutting in bright sunlight. High on each side, solid, green with a vivid green as glittering as snakes, rose what he took to be the famous jungle, sheer from the red-banked earth. He climbed down to the track. The train lay along the lines, vulnerable as a broken-backed caterpillar; the wall of leaves glittered as with a million hidden eyes. He was close to the head of the train; by the locomotive, a railway official was arguing with the dismounted Malay driver.

'He says it is dangerous to go farther. Many drivers have been killed. He is frightened.'

That the driver was frightened was obvious; his dark eyes seemed to be trying to see all ways at once, even out of the back of his head. His dark head shook as the official said that he must go on. His hands wiped themselves ceaselessly on an oily piece of rag. No. He was not going on. He was frightened.

Holl came leaping up. 'Of course he's going on,' he said.

'But,' said the official, 'I don't see what more we can do. He will be dismissed, of course, but he says he does not care – '

'You forget,' said Holl, gaily, 'there's a war on.' He pulled out his revolver, and looked at the driver with an eye of benevolent murder. 'Uppety!' he said, beckoning with the barrel. 'You mustn't be frightened; you'll be all right. Uncle Sam is coming with you.'

The man opened his mouth to scream, and Holl wrapped an arm swiftly but tenderly about his face, motioning upwards with the gun. 'Giddy-up,' he said. 'There's a good lad. I've always wanted to be an engine driver.'

The train proceeded towards its destination, which was, as Scrapings duly announced at a conference in his carriage, the town of Malacca, some hundred and fifty miles north-west of Singapore, on the west coast, and over a hundred miles south of any fighting so far. The battalion sorted itself out in its quarters, based on a school building by a fairly large open area beyond the outskirts of the town. The first day, Alan spent in discouragement with his platoon; they had by now got his wireless drill word- and knob-perfect, but once the sets were turned on, and the voices came out of them at the men out of nothing, they forgot everything and turned every knob with the abandon of an amateur organist improvising and pulling every stop in sight. Alan, who could only be with one set at a time, went almost berserk until he had closed them into a manageable ring, but by then they were bored and stupid. He returned dispirited, to find Sundar Singh fiddling with his kit.

His orderly announced that B Echelon, which had been making its separate way from Singapore by road, had arrived. He seemed thoughtful. At length he said, in a swift rush, that B Echelon had passed many other road convoys, all going in the opposite direction. They had even, in a railway siding near a town, seen a hospital train; it had been machine gunned, they said, from the air. They also said that the Japanese had tanks. Have we got tanks, sahib?

Of course we have tanks. Alan was taken by surprise. The tanks were no doubt being held in reserve, he said.

And aeroplanes? They said the sky 'up there' was thick with aeroplanes, but none of them were ours.

'You saw the fine aeroplanes over the ship when we sailed into Singapore. Those were ours.'

'Yes, sahib.'

'Well?'

Sundar Singh was still uneasy. 'They say, sahib, the Japanese take no prisoners.' With an odd furtive look around him, he gestured vividly as one having his throat cut.

Alan looked at his orderly. The brown liquid eyes looked back at him with the question. Alan turned his face away, and directed it to the wall; he felt it set in sad, stern, mortuary lines.

'It may be,' he said to the wall, 'that the Japanese are a barbarous, uncivilised – ' His statement became too theoretical for his Urdu to cope with; what was the Urdu for uncivilised? He felt very uneven, and exasperated. In a hard cold voice, he said: 'It need not concern us, Sundar Singh. If they do that, there is no reason why we should not do that too.'

With large, wondering eyes, his orderly looked at him.

'And, of course, we shall not *be* taken prisoners.'

His orderly said nothing, but looked.

Alan turned away and said masterfully: 'Now I have to attend a conference. Is there a clean shirt?'

'Yes, sahib. There is a clean shirt.'

The conference dealt with routine matters. Scrapings was fresh from another conference at Brigade Headquarters. The brigade was disposed thus and thus; routine training would continue, and the fighting companies must take every advantage of this respite to get used to working in rubber and in jungle; but he had to remind his officers that all ranks must be continuously on the alert. One company, with transport, was always to be ready to go out at a moment's notice to deal with any alarm. The Japanese were believed to have no transport vessels on this coast – indeed, how could they, seeing that they had attacked on the other coast and had no access by sea to this side? – while certain areas were mined, and the whole patrolled by the Navy, but there always remained the possibility of small infiltrations by night in native craft. Any such would be mopped up forthwith. On land, added Scrapings, Japanese troops were certainly infiltrating in extremely unorthodox fashions like (he quoted the G.O.C. Malaya) gangsters. On bicycles, for example, in civilian dress. Any such bicyclists encountered would be shot on sight. He spoke on...

It was really, Alan decided privately, a myth. Out of the window he could see palm trees that drooped elegantly across an evening sky where colour ran and fused in a most carefully contrived sunset. It was all a myth.

Scrapings had arrived at a pause. Then he said, heavily: 'It has been proved, I regret to report, in the course of this campaign that the Japanese do not take prisoners.' He paused again. His grey moustaches twitched. 'It would be unjust to our men to conceal this from them, but' – his voice dropped – 'this... this *perverse* information may also bolster our own morale, our own determination. I think you should make it clear to your men that – there is, of course, no official directive possible on this point – but you should make it plain to your men that what the Japanese can do, we can do too.

Gentlemen, two can play at any game.'

His audience received this in silence. Alan looked round at the sad faces, and felt himself very sad too. Yet at the same time his mind bridled, and irresponsibly he almost neighed: *Except certain kinds of patience*. But at the same time he heard the echo of his own voice saying likewise, in almost the same words, to his orderly and across it an unheeded dribble of thought like a ticker tape: *This is not reasonable; this is not civilised; there is no reason to panic...* None of these messages cohered into audible words, and his face remained mutely sad.

Scrapings asked for questions.

Holl signalled. He had many questions. To begin with, for his own company at least, he wished to ask for an immediate issue of gym shoes; the army boot, he said, could be heard coming a mile off in jungle or rubber, and it was also difficult to climb trees in boots.

'Climb *trees*?' said Scrapings, with a hint of exasperation.

Holl said that it was obvious that one had to take every advantage that the terrain afforded. There were a remarkable number of trees – ideal, for example, for sniping.

'*Ex*-cellent point, Holl,' said Scrapings. Malacca would be rifled of gym shoes the next day. Holl continued with his queries.

Next morning Alan was sent downtown with a truck and the quartermaster to shop for gym shoes. An air raid warning coincided with his arrival, and the truck was brought to a halt by what felt like the whole of Asia evacuating from the town. Alan parked the truck under a tree, and sat down to wait. One plane went over very high, too high to distinguish its breed, and nothing happened except a fragmentary shower of paper. Alan collected a few, but they were all in Malay or Chinese. Then Sundar Singh came up with one that showed a British officer crouching under shelter while Indian troops fought despairingly in front.

Sundar Singh asked what it was.

Alan explained that the British officer was himself, while Sundar Singh was one of the Indian troops.

With his mouth open, Sundar Singh looked at the crude drawing. When he had worked it out, he turned his eyes, worried, on Alan, who explained it again.

Sundar Singh had a brainwave. He pointed to the men fighting. 'You, sahib,' he said, '*there*. And me here.' He pointed to the man in shelter, and giggled.

'O.K.,' said Alan. 'But when you've finished cleaning my shoes there, you come out and help me fighting in front.'

Sundar Singh agreed to this, and took the pamphlet off to explain to his colleagues.

This was the first Japanese plane they had seen.

After a while the residents of the town began to seep back, and soon the shops were open again, and Alan went about commandeering, against universal protest, such stocks of rubber shoes as he could find. Storekeepers were reluctant to believe that his signature would be redeemable against money, and he felt that he was probably missing large concealed stores; such shoes as there were would be, he guessed, too small for most of his large-footed troops.

In the afternoon he turned to his platoon again, who were still hopelessly embroiled in the delicate mysteries of wireless communication. Suddenly, just before they had to stop for the day, everybody got the hang of it almost simultaneously. In a state almost of exaltation, with rapt expressions, they walked about chanting harshly across the air from one set to another. Scrapings appeared while they were doing this, and was moved to praise Alan; it was the first time he had spoken to, rather than at, Alan since the incident on board ship.

'Invaluable,' he said. 'May well be vital. And what range will we work at?'

Alan said that with luck the range would cover any normal dispersal that a battalion might expect, but that working in rubber might somewhat reduce the efficiency of the sets; that he would have to try it out the next day. Accordingly, he set forth next morning to a big rubber plantation, where he disposed his sets. They switched on. Not a signal came through. After checking for faults and finding none, Alan moved the sets closer. As the morning wore on, and the green gloom lightened beneath the climbing sun, he at last established contact at between a hundred and two hundred yards. His men, triumphant again, smiled across at him, as they said *Ack Company to Don Company over*, and understood nothing of the implications.

Straightening up, Alan found himself looking into the eyes of his havildar. Then he looked away, and all around him the trees stretched away like an ordered maze of bars under the roof-thick leaves. Visibility, he reckoned, was just about the range of his wireless sets. Then he felt the trees like a hostile cordon ringed about them; his signallers, aware at last that something was wrong, fell silent. Wildly, he looked around him, as the threat behind each tree trunk seemed to move. He forced himself to look back at his havildar.

'*Ultimately*,' he said. 'In the end, they are no good. I am sorry.'

Expressionless, the havildar looked at him. 'In the end,' he said, we still have the field telephones, the flags.'

'In the end,' said Alan, 'we have our good thick legs, and our loud voices.'

The havildar grinned suddenly, and glanced with a derisive hawk at the sets, intimating that he had never thought, himself, that this new-fangled trash could work anyhow.

'O.K., havildar sahib. Now all we've got to do is find the bloody trucks and we can all go home.'

As they were piling into their trucks, Scrapings came alongside in a station wagon. Alan broke the news to him, and his commanding officer went purple, controlling himself with obvious difficulty. After a little wordless bubbling, he said: 'We'll have a word about this later, Mart.' Not in front of the men, his bleak eye said, eloquent with contempt. 'In the meantime, we must try to work out other methods of communication; it's a major problem, when we're likely to be operating in small detachments at long range. Mustn't we, Mart?' Well, said his eye, go on, Mart; think of something.

'Drums, sir,' said Alan fiercely. 'We might be able to work something out with native drums.'

The glaring eyes popped, and blinked rapidly. Then they glazed with a wary caution. Alan saw Scrapings' gaze wander and tangle in angry lost bewilderment amongst the endless trees, and, recognising the feeling, his own anger vanished as suddenly he felt the full weight of responsibility on those elderly thin shoulders.

'We'll think of something, sir,' he said gently but confidently.

Later that day, a message reached him from the C.O. He was to proceed at once into Malacca again, and corner all native drums that might be available.

In the Mess that evening, as they ate hurriedly in between business, the officers were preoccupied. Rumours of a major engagement were coming through from the Slim River position. Holl came in late, sweating and weary, and plumped down silent at Alan's side.

After a while he said: 'They don't like it, you know. All those bloody trees moving around them all the time. They keep on looking over their shoulders as if something was going to jump on 'em from behind.'

Alan told him about the wireless sets, and, when he had finished eating, took him and showed him his hoard of drums. Holl looked at them blearily.

'You're a bloody fool, aren't you, Alan?'

'Yes.'

Holl stared at him, and then, bored, thought of other things. 'I've done for today. Maybe we ought to go and paint Malacca red. Last chance we'll get, I should say.'

'I'm not painting anything red with you. Not even a pillar box.'

But Holl was suddenly illuminated by the idea of pleasure and of city lights; he swept Alan off almost physically to the adjutant. The adjutant agreed with Alan, and besought Holl to be reasonable but in the middle of his pleadings Scrapings appeared. To him, Hol appealed directly.

Scrapings thought; he seemed to be working up to an explosion and Alan could feel the reminder coming that they were sti technically under open arrest, when Scrapings' eye fell on th adjutant, and softened. 'Bill,' he said, 'you've been on the job twent hours a day for five days solid now. It's time you had a break; yo go with them. Holl; Mart. No nonsense. No whisky. Understand No trouble.'

With a somewhat indignant adjutant aboard, Alan and Ho drove through the lampless dark; on their right was the sea, cal and silver under the moon, remote as peace beyond the blac inclination of the palm trees. Briefly, as the truck floated past, Alan doted on this remoteness; he would have liked to stop, to brood over it, to strip and swim in it; it would, he was thinking confusedly, be cleaning, it might even be Lethe. But he was already following Holl into the dimly lighted smoky confusion of a dance hall; as they came in the band faltered, and the people's heads turned in the thick light to look. The officers sat at a table, and drank warm fizzy beer, while everyone looked at them. To Alan their eyes, their expressions, were inscrutable; he knew only that he was intruding. But Holl, impervious to stares, was studying form. Having studied, he made his choice, and rose. With a thin dark Chinese taxi-girl in red trousers, he danced, working vigorously about her like a village dancer round a maypole. The stares seemed to become less concentrated, but Alan could still sense, almost as palpable as the smoke-fog, the continuing impassive curiosity about him; they were, he thought, as bad as the trees in the rubber plantations; waiting, watching.

Holl came back, sweating. She was, he said, a good girl, but dear. Twenty-five cents a dance. He drank a lot of beer. Alan, who had been contemplating with interest one girl who was taller than the rest, and with more flesh, rose to dance. In his arms, she was less substantial than she had looked, and flat as a board.

Her name, she said, smiling brilliantly, was Susie. Her mouth opened and shone over teeth; her eyes shone over nothing, shallow and troubling, and in them he saw his own face.

'But your Chinese name?'

She was indignant. She was not Chinese; she was British.

Conversation flagged. Alan rested his cheek on her hair, and she was still more indignant. They danced, mechanically, distantly, to *Begin the Beguine*. When Alan returned to his table, twenty-five cents the poorer, he found Holl alone. A message had come for the adjutant; the brigadier was on his way over. 'Not a flap,' said Holl, yawning. 'They don't want us. I've promised to keep off the whisky. Also I promised for you, you dangerous drunk.' He swirled a glassful of a pale liquid of a dubious yellow-amber tinge.

'What's that?' said Alan.

'They *say*,' said Holl, 'that it's whisky. But they know bloody well, and I know bloody well, that it's nothing of the sort, so that's all right, isn't it?'

Alan sipped at Holl's glass, and spat hurriedly. 'You damn' fool!'

'Yes,' said Holl. 'But only just this one. It's a crying scandal. Someone's got to try it so's to warn the troops off it. Go blind, I dare say.' He tutted briskly, whistled, took another sip and sucked at his teeth. 'Some alcoholic content, at any rate. That's what makes it so dangerous for young inexperienced drinkers.' He drained it and advanced with a gorilla-like stance upon the floor. Alan did not dance any more, but sat like a watchdog over Holl's glass, and Holl began to get sour. Eventually, he had an argument with one of his partners, and came flouncing back in disgust.

'Bloody nonsense!' he growled as he sat down. Almost immediately he stood up again. 'I know a whore when I see one,' he said. 'Just you wait here, laddie. I've a complaint to lodge with the management.' He shook off Alan's restraining hand. 'Don't be so *boring*, boy. I'm all right; in full possession of all my senses. *Too* full. I want service. I'll be right back.'

'What on earth...?' But Holl had gone. He was talking to a smoothly rounded Chinese in a tuxedo; this was presumably the manager and he began by looking very insulted. Then Alan saw him smile, and then with a quick gesture he opened a door behind him and he and Holl had vanished through it, before Alan had done more than stiffen with apprehension.

Uneasily, Alan twitched and sat, and watched the door. Unconsciously, his hand groped for and found his revolver butt; it rested there. Holl seemed to be away hours, and Alan was just working out how to rush the door that Holl had gone through when it opened and he reappeared. He was cheerful.

'Come on,' he said, beckoning. 'We're off. I've got a hot tip.'

Holl drove, refusing to explain any further; he probed cautiously out of town, but not in the direction of the camp.

'If you don't tell me where we're going,' said Alan, seriously worried at last, 'I'm getting out and I'll walk home.'

Holl laid a finger on the side of his nose, and leered appallingly in the moonlight. A strong reek came on his breath.

'Holl, what did you drink with that Chinese?'

'That pimp,' said Holl, 'has in's office bottles and bottles – but *bottles* of only the best Scotch, the true life-blood. Much as I should have liked to've refused, in view of maintaining desir'ble amic'l r'lationships with the native population, I could not. Could I?'

'Oh *God*!' said Alan. 'Come on. Switch over. I'll drive you back to camp.'

'Don't be stupid!' said Holl, swatting Alan's hand off the wheel. ''V'an urgent appointment. Besides, we can't turn here; be reasonable.' Nor could they turn: the truck was crawling now along a narrow track, scarcely wider than itself, with trees and thick undergrowth solid on the one side, and on the other the dark, glinting, stagnant water of the irrigation canal, the *parit*.

'As soon as we can turn, we turn,' said Alan, but with a sinking resignation of despair. He began to think, without much confidence, of ways and means of knocking Holl out without maiming him seriously.

The track seemed to go on for ever.

'You know we're already under open arrest.'

'Why, so we are!' said Holl, swerving dangerously. 'Well, isn't that nice. To know someone's looking after us; someone *cares*.'

The track had suddenly widened; Holl brought the truck slowly and majestically round in a half-circle to stop in the middle of a clearing. On one side the track continued, edged with the cold glint of the *parit*. Opposite was a row of low palm-thatched Chinese houses, bleached by the moon and shuttered tight against it. They looked fragile and shallow as a stage set, with the arching top-tufted palms splayed behind their roofs. Beyond them, the track narrowed to a mere path along the *parit* amongst clumps of bananas with ragged drooping leaves like banners of a broken army.

Holl switched the engine off. The two men sat there, and the silent moonlight was taut as a flood, calm yet known to be swelling, along the top of a dyke. Nothing moved, but the shadows by the houses and under the trees seemed inhabited, though the houses themselves were dead behind their blank faces.

'House on the far left, I think,' said Holl, in a confidential calculating whisper. 'Rum job. *Very* rum job. Not where I'd expect a lux-yourious high-class knocking shop... Just do a recce.' He swung down from the truck, and was over by the houses before Alan had taken in what he had said. Suddenly he realised that Holl was after a brothel. For the first time since they had left Bombay Alan laughed, but the shadows seemed to stir angrily, and an indignant hiss from Holl cut off his laughter. He watched Holl as he felt like a blind man over the front of the far house; then a door opened, a tiny slit of primrose-yellow light in the ashy moonlight. After a querulous buzz of muttering argument, the door opened a little wider, blinked, and closed suddenly. Holl had gone in.

Alone in the silent clearing, Alan sat under the moon. He tried to imagine Holl in there, but he could not believe the house had any inside. He thought of brothels, but they were ridiculous places. He had to stop the laughter again. There was one, he remembered, off the rue de Lappe, the long bar running down the long long room. There was the Madame in traditional black bombazine at the till; there were the women idling about like hens, desultory after feeding, sometimes naked, sometimes with a piece of gauze or two here or there. He was sitting at the long bar with a naked girl on a high stool on his right (her eyes were less like polished rocks than most of them), and on his left a highly tightly dressed girl in spectacles who was a researcher in sociology and who kept on leaning across him to address the more earnestly the girl on his right. Obviously, she was saying, the social security angle was not so good – she was interrupted by a brief sharp skirmish as Alan repelled the hand from his right that was infiltrating into his trouser pocket – but what she really wanted to know, in that husky-sweet deep Virginian voice, was, did the girls really find the work interesting?

He leaped in the seat of the truck like a hooked fish his hand skittering inexpertly for his gun.

'Dreaming again!' said Holl jovially. 'You'll be the death of us all one of these days. There are times, Alan, when it seems to me you'd have done better to apply for some staff job. The gold tooth glinted. 'Now; this is serious. There's only two of 'em there. A peach of a crumpet, all eyes, and shy. And then there's Aunt Jemima. I bagged the young one. After all, first come, first served, eh, old boy?'

His laughter made them both jump.

'And how old's Jemima?'

'Ah well,' said Holl, with a finger along his nose. 'We must be charitable. Say thirty-five? Thirty in the shade. Never can tell actually with these chinks. But game, lad. Game.'

'Toss you for it,' said Alan.

'My *God*!' said Holl. 'You're *sordid*. Come on, now, climb out of that truck. We'll have to look slippy. Better take off the distributor head, what? Nothing in the truck pinchable? All proper precautions?' His leering whispers scurried away into the shadows. 'What are we waiting for?'

Alan tried to explain that he did not, personally, find Chinese women fascinating. His idea of heaven was a large nordic blonde, like a honey-coloured sofa for relaxation.

Holl started to argue, mulish.

'Oh, for Christ's sake!' said Alan, suddenly exasperated, 'get along and do your duty as an officer and a gentleman. Then we can all go home to bed.'

Holl drew himself up stiffly. 'If that's the way you look at it, you bloody little prig, that's exactly what I shall do and good day to you.' He stood looking at Alan haughtily, then sketched a salute, and lurched over towards the far house. The door opened again, and he vanished. Almost immediately the door swung wide again, and out of an eldritch scream a slight figure in pale trousers fled from the house, and disappeared into the shadow back of the houses. Electrified, baffled, Alan saw Holl come out. He stood peering about a little, and then came back towards Alan.

He was cross. 'Bloody little *flirt*. Which way did she go?'

Alan indicated the direction the girl had not gone. Holl went clattering clumsily amongst the banana leaves, and then came back again. 'Not a hope.' He was morose. 'She'll be in Singapore by now.' He swore copiously, and then stood reflecting. 'Aunt Jemima it must be, then. Just as well you didn't – ' He leaned on the truck, and thought a bit. 'Just as well, he said eventually. 'Well. Bye-bye for now. I shan't be long.'

Once again the door of the Chinese house shut behind him. This time it stayed shut. In Alan's stomach a slow spiralling movement began to turn and to lift. He considered it carefully. It was like nausea, but it was not. He diagnosed it; it was laughter. He would have nothing to do with it and restraining a bucking motion of his head that wished to throw up and bray to the sky, he quelled it; it was hysteria. His hands trembling, he lit a cigarette. After the spurt of the match, the wide-eyed silence settled back again to stare at him. The little row of houses stood there, hollow and dead; nothing could live in there except cobwebs, and spiders big as rats jerking every now and then in the silted dust. Holl would never come out again; the elderly lady was a Japanese spy in no disguise, answering the obscene nakedness of Holl with naked knives. In the soft deep shadows with the sharp edges lurked violence.

Alan wiped his forearm across his sweating face; a sickly lemonish odour clung to him. It was only his anti-mosquito cream but it clung as close as gas. It was difficult to breathe, and breathing, he coughed, and shook the edges of the clearing like canvas scenery. His cough had split the silence open, and it roared, composed now of the voices of a million frogs, through whose bass thunder came suddenly the warning of a high-pitched treble drum. Thrice it beat, and the last beat was introductory to some statement, or herald of some tremendous entry. But nothing happened. After a gap, the three notes struck again, and again left the world suspended on its last beat. Alan's flesh began to creep; his fingers clenched. The shadows were advancing with supreme stealth, shrinking then clearing. Then the three notes rang again, and this time with relief he recognised them as a bird, the Fever Bird, the Knocking on the Ice bird that cannot let the darkness be.

He dragged deeply on his cigarette, and scornfully exhaled. But still he was sweating, and the sweat, acrid with mosquito cream, stung his eyes; the silence built up again beneath the roar of frogs. He thought, wilfully, of Holl, involved in there in his travesty of the last intimacy, and hurriedly he pushed the thought out – it was too vivid. He thought of Lettice; laying his palms on his chest, he summoned the thought of Lettice. It occurred to him, behind shut eyelids, not un-gratifyingly, that he had been very loyal to Lettice; he hadn't made love to anyone, apart from a perfunctory expected kiss here and there in the way of war-work, since he had left England. Thirteen months ago. He thought, concentrating, that he loved her; clenching his eyelids, he trawled for her in his darkness. His thought came up, empty, yet radiant. Sparks of fire hurt his closed eyes, and his lips moved:

So in a voice, so in a shapeless flame,
Angels affect us oft, and worshipped be;
Still when, to where thou wert, I came,
Some lovely glorious nothing did I see...

Somewhere on another plane, a thin pedagogic voice simultaneously contradicted this; Lettice, it said, had no existence in this Malayan night, though admittedly she might have, on the other side of the world, on the Backs in the November river-mist where the naked willows wept, for example, in someone else's arms perhaps, in someone else's mind perhaps. He frowned fiercely upon this, his head lifting, his nostrils dilating to apprehend her; they had a strange desultory rhythm when they walked together, bumping every now and then, touching by necessity. So, her hand would rest on his wrist...

In the hunched seat of the truck, he froze, his heart poised on the edge of silence like a stopped clock. Then he groaned from his stomach in pain, and said '*Lettice*!' And almost in the same split second, jerking furiously up in the seat, to the abominable horse-playing Holl, he burst out: 'You *bastard*!'

His hand, raised to smite Holl's hand off his wrist, stopped dead in mid-air. It was not Holl's hand; it was a small thin hand with long nails, laid light as a moth on his wrist; its owner was hissing softly for silence. At last, having survived, he looked up the arm, into the face of the girl in the pale trousers who had fled from Holl. She put her dark head on one side, flirtatiously, and smiled, and her hand moved in a fluttering caress on the skin of his arm. Dazed, he stared at her anonymous smiling face, the long oval under the smooth jet hair. Her eyes gleamed as she moved. She was speaking, very softly, with a lilt, with a humorous cajoling tinkle. Gradually, he understood that she wished him to come with her; her hand slid like a handle into his palm; her other hand slipped up into the hollow of his elbow, with infinite gentleness, and all at once he longed for her, so abruptly, so decisively that he had opened the truck door to get out before he realised what he was doing.

But the click of the door seemed to break something, and with a gasp the girl's hand was torn from his, and she was gone away into the shadows. As he stood there bewildered, he saw that it was not the click of the door that had put her to flight; it was the door of the far house that had opened, and Holl was coming over to the truck. He had not seen the girl, who had had the truck between him and her as she fled.

Holl climbed in. 'Gimme a cigarette.'

He seemed somewhat diminished, and in low spirits. Alan gave him a cigarette, automatically, and climbed in. He started the engine, turned the truck, its noise monstrous after so much silence, and engaged it again homewards on the narrow track between trees and water. When he had driven very carefully a little way, the spiralling movement began again in his stomach, and this time he could not control it. At first he giggled.

Holl, sucking fiercely at his cigarette, told him to cut it out.

With an effort, Alan subdued himself for the moment.

Holl, after some brooding, spoke. 'First it was the Poles and Czechs and all those randy Middle Europeans. Not to mention the Jews.'

He pursued his thoughts in silence for a while. Then he said heavily: 'And now – you realise, of course – those bloody Yanks'll be occupying England. And what sort of hope in hell d'you suppose any English girl has got with that lot around on the streets?' He paused a moment, and then burst out: 'By God! There are times when I think it's time this war packed up and we all went home.'

But the spiralling movement was whirling, out of control, through Alan's body. Clutching the wheel with both hands, doubled up over it, he burst, braying, with laughter. Swiftly Holl reached across him to jerk the truck clear of the water and stop it. He swore venomously.

'Get out! Cut that damn' cackling, and stick your head in the stream. *Move*!'

Alan reeled from the truck, and kneeling by the *parit*, heaving, thrust his head, bubbling and choking, into the water. It was thick, tepid and slimy; he lifted his head, and tears ran through the slime on his face. The noise had stopped, but the outraged whooping and howling still strained for escape at his ribs and lungs, and rang in his head. He stayed a little on his knees, mopping at his face with his handkerchief. Most of the slime came away, but the tears would not stop.

From the truck, Holl advised him impatiently to puke and get it over.

At last, in relatively good order, Alan was able to get back into the truck, where Holl had taken over the wheel. He said he was sorry, and Holl grunted, and started up. He drove staidly and soberly, occasionally groaning rather mechanically. Once or twice he glanced sideways at Alan, curiously, and finally said, with something of grudging envy in his voice: 'Where on earth did you get the booze from?' Alan did not answer, and there was no further conversation till they had almost reached the approach to their camp. Here Holl stopped the truck, and, climbing out, executed a surprise attack on the sentries. Then for five minutes, in a white-hot rage, he blew them up, ending by putting two of them under arrest.

As they drove on up to their quarters, Alan remonstrated, and was blown up in his turn. They were, Holl pointed out, on active service in a theatre of war; the troops had to be taught that this was not a game.

To quieten him, Alan apologised.

They stood in the moonlight. There was nothing left except to go to bed, but they hesitated.

'Good night, Holl,' said Alan.

'Good night,' and Holl turned. But after a few steps, he stopped.

'Alan.'

'Yes.'

'You might call me Sam.'

'Oh. Of course. I'm sorry. Good night, Sam.'

'Good night, Alan.'

FIVE

THAT SAME NIGHT, some one hundred and forty miles north of them, the Japanese tanks skittled eighteen miles through the carefully prepared British position at Slim River. The rumours of setback that reached Malacca in the course of the day hardened into news of catastrophe: yet another, and extremely comprehensive, skilful withdrawal was taking place. Late in the evening Holl viewed a map sourly, and commented that he couldn't see a line that anyone could hope to hold before the line Muar-Segamat-Mersing.

'Which,' said Holl, sourly, 'is twenty miles south of us. Twenty flipping miles *behind* where we now are.'

Yet a curious unreal peace held through Malacca for the next few days; the battalion sweated at martial exercises, dealt vainly with various alarms that all proved unfounded, and prepared at least three defensive positions. Then the forward troops began to come back through them in driblets, by night mostly, like ghosts or at best like embodied rumours, while the names of evacuated towns sounded ever nearer down the peninsula. But nothing seemed to disturb the depths of the strange calm of the coast that was suddenly only a quarter inhabited. One company was always in the town, to prevent looting, but hardly anything happened; few aeroplanes were seen, and there was hardly any direct attack from the air and none at all on Alan's battalion, which assumed in the flux an odd stability. Odd officers and groups of troops were always passing through and stopping off, storytelling in tired, strained voices with a matter-of-factness that carried only a dreamlike conviction. Presently one would wake up.

One hot afternoon a green-and-yellow camouflaged estate wagon came in fast up to the Battalion Headquarters, and an officer got out, a major from a British infantry unit, hatless, with a dry and dirty stubble. He demanded a bathroom. Alan was able to offer him this, and having installed him he came out again and was looking idly at the officer's car, which was somehow unusual. He realised that it had a great many small holes in it. He could not help putting a finger in one of the holes, and as he did so, he looked up at the sky involuntarily, and shivered.

A little later Holl appeared with another officer, an elegant, dandiacal creature with pressed shirt and shorts, and ankle puttees welded above dapper boots; he had a face as sharp as a racing prow, and he spoke with the precise, clipped authority of highly disciplined automatic fire. With a shock, Alan realised that this was the major who had gone in to bathe, emerged as from a chrysalis.

'A pretty contrast,' the major was saying, waving a hand at some of the battalion's trucks that stood by, dispersed under trees; their yellow desert camouflage looked bright and gay against the deep green of the foliage. 'Very *preh*-tty! I take it you were bound for the desert, but were–ah –interrupted. Let's see. You landed when?'

'Eleven days ago,' said Holl. 'Sir.'

The major turned to look at him. 'Ah. Ah well.' He put his hands behind his back, bounced on his toes slightly, and his eyelids fell to like a sleeping doll's. The sharpness of his face was the stretch of strain and fatigue, and he seemed to have set some inner mechanism to work to get the eyelids up again. He succeeded, and smoothed his smooth hair.

'Would you mind,' he commanded politely, 'showing me that position you were talking about? I'm sorry your C.O.'s not around, but you'll present my compliments, of course. I might be able to give you a tip of two, if you wouldn't think that unduly offensive – but it's tiresome country till you get the hang of it. They come down the road through the rubber or jungle, you see, until they contact; then they'll fan out and move round you, so you have to stagger back in defence outwards, so's you can take 'em on one shoulder after another. Otherwise they'll be round you in a jiffy and have a roadblock up behind you in no time. And you must keep your eyes and ears skinned for tanks. Mind you, they're quite human, these Nips, though you don't want to underrate them, ha ha. Bonny wee fighters, but not, we've found, not overfond of the bayonet. We'll go in my car...' His eyelids had dropped again, and he appeared to somnambulate into the car.

'You'll excuse the draughts,' he was saying, as the car moved off, and Alan glimpsed Holl's face as he sat beside the major. It was as sulky as a schoolboy's, unwilling under instruction. When he came back, alone, an hour later, his face was positively sultry.

Scrapings came back almost simultaneously from Brigade, cross and twitching; immediately he summoned his company commanders. As a precaution they were to take up the position astride the road that night.

Alan, getting bored later that evening with waiting for the battalion to move off, scouted forward to where Holl was awaiting the order to move. He found him squatting on the ground with his subadar, and asked him what the major had had to say.

Holl spat. 'Good bloke. Best that Sandhurst can sell. According to his batman, that bloke driving his car, he split a Nip officer in half with his own sword two days ago, which is all very healthy and good for the troops.' He sucked at his teeth, and spat again. 'Good officer. Good soldier. Knows his onions. Can't say I took to him. Just couldn't stand the sight of him, that's all. Knows too many brigadiers by their Christian names. Too bloody gallant.' He rumbled obscurely, and then said with lucid emphasis: 'What I mean to say is, if you stick a bayonet into a man's guts and fork 'em out, by God you *fork*! All that lah-di-dah.'

'Oh.'

Holl sniffed. '*Bash* 'em!' he said, ruffling, and scrabbled in some grass. Then he changed tack abruptly. 'If it rains tonight,' he said, 'I shall lay me down and die.' He sounded peevish now as an old woman.

It was almost dark, and Alan squatted in the hot clutch of the night. He thought coolness and rain might be cause enough to lay down a life for, and said so.

Holl swore, contrary. 'That's enough of that. I lay down my life for nobbut and for nobody. I don't hold with all this laying.'

'All the best war memorials,' said Alan, meditating. 'I mean lots of chaps seem to lay – '

'Utt's not for joking.'

'Polished granite,' said Alan, heedless. Suddenly he was light in the head, dangerously so as he had been with Holl in the truck. Vividly he could see the dapper major, in pressed bronze uniform, one knee forward, one Boer-War-type rifle menacing the prosperous peaceful city centre. He giggled. 'They'll squeeze us into a P.S. Bulk consignment, *also in memory of all those who...* Cut small, though. Because no room. They won't *build* any new ones.'

A runner coming up, hoarse and confidential and sweating, interrupted him. They were moving. Holl gave his orders, and automatically in the blind dusk his huge arm moved, and forward.

They went easily enough into their prepared position; retiring troops went through them occasionally in sparse convoys with a faltering blink of hooded lights, and presently their brigadier arrived and held conference. By some time next day there would be nothing between the battalion and the Japanese advance. The brigadier said they must have no illusions about the nature of their task; it would be tough and bloody. His voice was male, firm and tough, rasping on the soft night air. His orders were that the position would be held to the last man and the last round.

Unbelieving, Alan watched the dawn awake in the leaves above; it curdled, green, and at last came dappling down on the naked ground between the naked mottled trunks of the rubber that lifted twenty feet, it seemed, before they branched. They were planted regularly in rows, wide enough, as they had been warned, to allow tanks free passage. Unbelieving still, Alan waited for tanks to claim free passage. His telephone wires were out, his companies lucidly interlocked, the troops quiet in their weapon pits. Everyone was all set to wait. To the south a cock was crowing intermittently, yet urgently, as though to recall something that someone had for gotten. All day long they waited, but the only troops that came from their front were still odd detachments of British troops. It seemed that we had blown up many bridges, but no one seemed to have seen the enemy for a long time, nor to know where they actually were.

At last an order came through from Brigade; they were not to fight to the last man and the last round after all – at least not here. They were to withdraw, some twenty miles down the coast, south of the River Muar.

Duly they withdrew, at night also, but now in torrential rain, down a road like a canal through black banks of trees. In the humid grey-green first light, they moved in driblets by ferry across the river and then inland in a wilderness of trees, and again into position astride a road that was apparently identical with the one they had left, in the raining rubber. There for four days they stayed.

The morning after they moved in Scrapings attended another conference at Brigade, and returned with the news, not altogether unexpected, that this position too was to be held to the last man and the last round. Later, Alan studied maps with Holl in a stern attempt to discover where they were and what they had to hold so finally. The brigade, three battalions strong, less than three thousand men, were occupying twenty-five miles – as the crow flies – of meandering river in country thickly covered with jungle or rubber. The line of the river itself, which was to be denied to the enemy, was nearer fifty miles; on their left flank the brigade was also to hold an undefined length of sea coast. Alan's battalion was forward, on the left centre, with another battalion ten miles away forward on the right centre. The third battalion was nominally in reserve, but in fact guarding the river mouth and the coast. The brigade's artillery had not come with them from India because it did not exist, but a battery of Australian 25-pounders were promised in support, and two Australian battalions and also, it was rumoured, anti-tank guns were said to be moving up into positions behind them.

Alan grasped all this and looked at the map – at the thin irresolute line which was the river and at the vivid green patches which were jungle. He looked up from the map at the solid bare trunks that dwindled away from them but nevertheless closed their sight at a radius of a hundred yards or so. They seemed like prison bars arrayed wilfully as a maze. It seemed to him that one could not hope within reason to hold country like this without much less than a man per tree, and he looked to Holl to say so, but swallowed the remark. Holl stood at his side in a shaft of sun; he was wet through from the night's rain, and he steamed in the sunlight, smoking like an expended firework. Indeed he seemed almost to be evaporating as he stood, the skin shrinking and withering into the contours and gullies of his face and neck, so that he looked suddenly an old man. His eyes blinked against the light, and the corners of his mouth drew down; he looked not merely old, but tired, not merely tired, but worn-out. Quickly, Alan shifted his ground. I profile Holl looked all right, just wet and warm, but in that moment it had been for Alan as though all the circling trees had taken one vast silent stride in upon them. His heart beat heavy and jerking, and his ribs could not give it enough room; suddenly and sickly, he felt his flesh deciduous upon the bone.

Holl was lifting up his face as if in prayer to some hostile presence in the sky. '*Hit* 'em,' he said, sullenly. 'Hit 'em where we find 'em; if only to God we could find 'em before they find us.'

And they were now, in fact, at last, the front line, and still nothing happened. They threaded slinking patrols endlessly across the miles of rubber, as though darning an ever-unravelling hole. At night, half of them stood to, while the other half slept or at least lay, and at night, too, the monsoon rain came down with a majestic roar upon their roof of leaves, and each leaf tilted its separate cascade on the men beneath. The troops existed in a damp stupor, rousing to cross pleasure only when the cooking fires were lit in the respite from rain. To the west they could sometimes hear the earnest sound of war as the bombers stood over the town of Muar, but they hardly ever saw a plane through the vertical shafts up through the trees, where the cloud hung grey on the wet green.

On the fourth day, in the afternoon, the clouds vanished altogether and there was continuous bombing over Muar for two hours. Then Alan was ordered to take some men down to the road that left southwards from Muar. He was to check the refugees crowding out of the bombed town; from them he was to filter all fifth-columnists and infiltrating Japanese.

A thought struck him. 'How do I recognise fifth-columnists and Japanese from Chinese?'

Scrapings looked at him coldly. 'Infiltrators mostly, according to report, are on bicycles and wear khaki shorts and white singlets. But the essential point is to use your intelligence, Mart.'

'Japanese,' said someone else, 'make a low, hissing noise when frightened.'

'They can't pronounce their *r's*. Make them say *right round and riddle-me-ree*. They have squarish heads and are short and sturdy whereas Chinks are long headed and weedy.'

'The great thing,' said the adjutant sagely, 'is their *toes*. If there's a *big* gap between his big toe and the next one he's a Jap. Shoot him.'

'For God's sake,' said Scrapings, 'don't do anything bloody idiotic.'

In the truck, the troops revived with the rush of air. Teeth shone in the brown faces, fierce eyes rolled at the trees and rifles bristled. In the front seat, Alan felt a touch from behind on his shoulder. He looked round. His orderly looked down at him, his round face in an extraordinary grimace mingling martial menace and juvenile gaiety; then he relaxed the grimace, and beamed.

Alan raised his eyebrows.

'*Thik hai*, sahib,' said Sundar Singh. 'O.K.' – and grinned yet more widely.

On the main road they turned towards Muar, and crawled through the exodus. There were men, women and children; Malays, Chinese, Tamils, Eurasians; all proceeding southwards in dogged motley, with carts, goats, pushcarts and innumerable bicycles. Most of those with bicycles were wearing khaki shorts and white singlets. Nearly every one wore an expression, fixed as a mask, of determined and sorrowful bewilderment. Their backs and their vehicles were laden with mattresses, suitcases, bundles, rolls of linoleum, fowls dangling by trussed claws, clocks, bags of rice, carpets, pillows, cooking pots and pans, umbrellas and babies. The stream parted sullenly before the blunt bows of the truck, and closed again beyond them; high in his seat, Alan floated as if against a tide of flotsam. After a few moments' silent astonishment, his men, from their advantage of height and solidarity of uniform and armament, began to find the spectacle amusing, and started to shout remarks.

By a cluster of houses they disembarked. Alan set up his interrogation centre in a Chinese sweet-shop. He had already explained their task to the men, modifying his instructions to a simple request that they pick up anyone they did not like the look of, with a special emphasis on bicyclists wearing khaki shorts and white singlets. Within two minutes he had at least twenty indignant bicycle owners queuing for questioning. None of them spoke any English, or at least none of them were letting on if they did. His havildar frisked them for arms, and looked at Alan for further orders. Alan looked at their faces. Dark brown in the slanting sockets, their eyes looked back at him with a cold surface sheen and below that a deep dark trouble that might be fear, that might be contempt. Sadly, utterly impotent, he looked in their eyes, and their dignity within their indignity confused him so much he could not think, but only feel the mute accusation of their protest like bats within his head.

How did one tell a square head from a long head? When was a long head short enough to be held square? He picked an ambivalent head at random, and indicated that its owner was to take his shoes off.

Then he jumped. He could have sworn that the man had said *Oh, go to hell*!

'What?'

But the man was speaking Chinese, in torrents which stopped most abruptly when Alan's havildar nudged him with his tommy-gun. The bicyclist sat down on the floor and took off his rather fanciful yachting sneakers; his hands trembled a little, and on one of his fingers was a heavy ring with a minute jade dragon set in the bezel. His feet emerged, with long delicate toes in the texture and colour of old ivory. Alan considered the distance between the great toe and its neighbour. They were, at least, separate. He told the havildar to hold that man.

But he had no idea what to do next. A small voice in the back of his head suggested more than once that the logical sequence was to play Hunt the Slipper, and he thought he'd better go out for a moment to try to clear his head.

To give himself direction, he proceeded smartly round the houses to make sure that the bright desert truck was properly under cover. To his astonishment, he ran into a beautifully camouflaged troop of light anti-aircraft guns. There were two blinking English sentries on guard, who motioned him to a hut, where he found a lieutenant flat on a table, his head lolling sideways, his blue and dirty chin tilted towards the roof, gulping as he snored. Alan stood over him; he looked as if he had not been out of his clothes for a long time. Then the chin snapped up in a gulp that was almost a choke; a pair of dead yellowish grey eyes swam up under the lids, and suddenly his whole body jumped like a hooked fish. Sitting up, his revolver in one hand, he looked fiercely foolish. 'What the hell are you?'

Alan told him.

The lieutenant pushed his hand wearily over his eyes. 'You've no right. Going round scaring people out of their wits. Not to mention out of the first kip they've had for two and a half days.'

A captain came into the room at speed. 'For Christ's sake!' he said, seeing Alan. 'Oh, never mind who the hell you are, I've not time. Jock, up you get! We're off again. Limber up.'

Groaning, the lieutenant found his feet. 'Not *again*! I can't bear it; two hundred miles we've done in a fortnight.' Then he was shouting orders out of the doorway as he heaved on his webbing. In the sunlight outside, he stood for a moment. 'I'm *tired*,' he said. Without speaking for a moment, he looked at Alan curiously; upright he had a rather sad almost wistful expression. Through a yawn, he said: 'Never have so many run so fast and so far from so few. Bye-bye, sonny. Keep your pecker up; see you in Singapore. Bless us all.'

In a moment he was back. 'For Christ's sake get that bloody yellow circus truck out of my light. It's bang in the way of my guns. I've got to *move*!'

Having shifted his truck, Alan went back to his interrogation station. He felt oddly abandoned, pointlessly stationary in the endless flow of refugees between the shuttered and empty houses of the little hamlet; nor had he advanced any further with the problem of identification of fifth-columnists. But, inside the hut, he found a strange white man of about fifty, with a round face floating over the khaki turbans of Alan's men, like a portly and superior bloom of tropical high living. He was talking to one of Alan's suspects with the bored precision of one dictating a routine letter to a secretary, but in fluent Malay. Catching sight of Alan, he saluted him smartly, and revealed himself clad incongruously in the uniform of a private. Alan was both suspicious and embarrassed, but as the stranger told him that he had been detailed off by the Volunteers to assist the battalion generally, as he was, in civilian life, a planter on a nearby estate and knew the whole district intimately, suspicion gave way to a warm relief, and he thanked God forcefully.

Some rather furtive-looking civil police had also appeared, and Alan understood that he could if he wished make over any suspects apprehended, if any, to them. With the planter, he reconsidered his captures to date, and detained two. The last one they spoke to was the man who had been made to remove his socks and shoes; he still sat on the floor with bare feet.

'Seen him before,' said the planter. 'Don't you run a wireless shop at Port Swettenham?'

The man's face flickered, but he said nothing.

'He doesn't speak English,' Alan explained. The man's bare feet embarrassed him, and he wanted to get rid of him.

The planter glanced sideways at Alan like a schoolmaster rebuking a member of the class who had interpolated a particularly foolish suggestion. 'Of course he speaks English.' He addressed the man again. 'I bought a wireless off you in thirty-eight – I used to have an estate up that way. Good wireless it was, too.'

The man swallowed, and then said, in excellent English: 'That is quite correct. I am sorry not to have answered the officer before, but I feared that if he knew I spoke English he might wish me to act as interpreter for him, and I wish, excuse me, to hurry on. My wife and family – '

'Silly ass!' said the planter. 'Might have got yourself in trouble. But I think we might let him go, sir. I mean if you think fit. Everyone knows him in Port Swettenham.'

His tone of voice seemed to imply to Alan that no one in his senses would have detained him in the first place, and Alan felt himself blushing. Crossly, he agreed. He watched the man as he laced his shoes, and saw his fingers trembling slightly and noticed again the heavy ring with the jade dragon on it. While his mind was groping confusedly with a suspicion that he could not put into words, he was annoyed again to find himself explaining as if in self-defence to the planter that he had been told the Japanese had big gaps between their big toe and their second toe.

The planter blinked, and said he had never heard of that. He looked sideways at Alan, rather oddly, and then asked abruptly when they were to 'down tools.'

The afternoon wore on; the stream of refugees wore on, apparently inexhaustible, until about five o'clock when suddenly there were no more. Alan, whose orders were to stay there until further instructions, walked restlessly up and down. He wondered why there were no more refugees; why there had been no aeroplanes that afternoon. He was within a mile of the town.

At last an orderly appeared on the empty road, looking lonely on his motor-cycle. They were to return immediately to base. As Alan crumpled the message form, and turned to his havildar, he tightened suddenly into immobility, listening. From the north-west, the direction of the town and the river mouth, a metallic almost tinny cackle dribbled into the silence like pennies into a beggar's empty cup. Alan felt something flutter behind his eyes.

Rather sharply he gave his orders to return to camp, but the end of the sentence was broken by bursts of firing, nearer than the last.

His havildar looked at him; his men looked at him. The planter, suddenly much redder even than before, had his head on one side and looked as if he was sniffing.

'*That*,' said the havildar, 'is ours. The first one was Them from the other bank of the river. Ha.'

Alan nodded calmly, as though this were all old stuff, and motioned the men towards the truck. In a renewed silence, they seemed to tiptoe, almost with reverence, towards the truck. The firing sounded again before they reached it and everyone got in rather hurriedly, standing scared-looking for a moment, and then grinning furtively. Swiftly the truck sped down the road, away from the noises. Abruptly Alan felt angry, and deceived, and began to say to the planter, squashed at his side in the front of the truck: 'I wish – ' He stopped.

'What's that?'

Alan had started to say, in fact, that he wished they did not have to *start* by going in the opposite direction from the firing. Instead, he said: 'Well, there we are.'

The tyres made an even rushing noise on the smooth tarmac. For all his straining ears, Alan could hear no further sounds of firing. He felt flat, as if he had been sick, and jumpy, and also resentful. Unreasonably, for this was what he had been preparing for by the long months at the Cadet College; by three months as an officer: conflict with the enemy. All up the peninsula men had been engaged in this conflict for some time. It was the order of the day; natural, and inevitable. Now, suddenly, inevitable as a tidal wave.

He swallowed, but his mouth was dry. He looked round, cautiously, at the inexpressive faces of his men; he wondered if they felt like he did. The plump red face of the planter had set in severe though soft lines, his fleshy mouth pursed a little, the lower lip thrust forward. He was whistling softly. Alan inclined slightly towards him. He discovered that the planter used an expensive after-shave lotion and that he was whistling, very softly, *Tea for Two*. Alan did not find this knowledge concerting. His thoughts seemed to be taking off like pigeons at the sound of a shotgun.

'Ah, well,' he thought firmly, suppressing them, 'here we are; here we all are.' He hitched his shoulders straight under his webbing, but as he did so he was appalled by a voice so loud in his head that he thought everyone in the truck must be able to hear it. It said: For Christ's sake what are you doing here? He coughed loudly, and peered fiercely at the side of the road to surprise any ambush. But all he saw was the shifting serried ranks of the rubber trees, and he seemed to have no answer at the moment to the voice's question.

Next morning, from their uneasy lines in the rubber, they heard the battle break at dawn some miles away. Their orders were to stay put, and to deal with anything coming down their road. Nothing came down their road. Except for the distant noise and some confused messages from Brigade, nothing at all happened all morning; nothing was certain, except that the Japanese were already across the river near its mouth.

A little later Alan was surveying his installations, dropping here and there what he hoped was a calm, cool encouragement, although he himself was jumping inside like frogs in a jar. It was the middle afternoon, the sky clouded, but sultry and oppressive. He returned to the road, to find Holl standing rigid as a monolith in front of Scrapings;

but Holl was not being rebuked. Four miles south-west, on the road connecting their position with Muar, the Japanese had established a roadblock; they were reported as being only a small force of some fifty or sixty men, and Holl was to take his company to destroy them and the block.

Holl was on one knee, with maps, establishing his position and his orders. He asked a few terse questions. His face was grey, his mouth a slot in its bleak wall, but his eyes shone. He stood up again, rigid now, and saluted. Alan saw him, as he adjusted his webbing, cast brief, loaded orders to his platoon commanders. As Alan watched, Holl seemed to change into a bulky, armoured instrument of war, his face anonymous between his puggree and his shirt collar. Alan saw him go off to his waiting troops; a few minutes later the trucks rushed past, accelerating hard, and out of sight down the road.

There was no noise to break the waiting for their return other than the rumble of distant battle that had been going all day; even that seemed to be quieting. The afternoon began to fade, and damp darkness to fill up between the tree trunks. Alan was down at the wireless truck, where one of the 'professional' signallers from Brigade was trying to take down a message. Three armoured cars had been allotted to them and should arrive very shortly. The report of the situation in the town was extremely vague, but Australians were moving up in support; Alan's unit was to establish contact with the Australians, and stand by for further orders. The operator was having trouble, and doubted, swearing, if he'd be able to maintain contact for long.

Down the road, sixty yards away in the gloom, came the noise, shockingly loud, of the returning trucks. By the time the message coming through on the wireless had been checked and Alan, running, had arrived at Battalion H.Q., Holl had finished speaking. He stood in the semi-darkness, in a little clearing just off the road; in front of him was a little group of silent officers. Scrapings turned from Holl in a savage thrust on his heel, and then swung back again; his hands made a sharp trembling gesture as if he were throwing something away. Then he took a step forward, and laid a hand on Holl's shoulder, gently. Alan saw Holl shake; he winced himself in sympathy and turned and walked blindly into the trees. He found himself standing over two sepoys in a slit-trench, saying '*O.K.*, *O.K.*,' to them in a stupid voice. He turned and went back and delivered the message to the adjutant.

Then he went to Holl. He found him as he was backing out of a low bivouac of ground-sheets on all fours. He waited till he was clear, and upright.

'Sam.'

Holl peered at him in the dark, and then looked away. His head was bare, and his webbing unlatched so that the ammunition pouches hung like aged breasts on his chest. His throat seemed to be moving.

'What happened?' Alan did not want to ask this but could not help himself.

'He never came,' said Holl. '*He never came*! Ah, the bastard the judas bastard.' He swore, gulping in breath between each expletive as if he had only just stopped running. It had been a classic attack, he said: text book. De-trucked, they had moved through rubber and sighted the enemy without being seen themselves. Almost to the rear of the enemy there was a rise in the ground. 'I sent him round; we synchronised. He had absolutely foolproof orders. All he had to do was to bring his platoon smack down on the rear as soon as we'd got their interest, and we had 'em cold. Couldn't have missed; there can't have been more than fifty of them there.'

'What happened?'

'He never came!' Holl's voice broke, and he sighed and sobbed with curses.

'He might have got lost. Perhaps he wasn't there on time.'

'A child of two couldn't have got lost.' Holl choked. 'He hadn't the guts. The stinking yellow bastard!'

Clumsily, Alan sought to comfort him. The platoon commander must have gone astray somehow, and anyway it was only a skirmish and the object of the operation had been achieved: the block had been cleared even if the enemy had escaped.

'He let me down. He let me down; he never came,' repeated Holl stubbornly.

Alan blundered on until he realised that Holl was not listening. He stopped. Holl was turned slightly from him, his legs apart, but lurched askew, with his head pressed on to one shoulder, his mouth open, a blotch on the pallor that was his face.

Horrified, Alan clasped his hands. Holl was jerking with dry spasmodic sobs deep in his throat.

At last, in a hoarse, shameful voice, Holl said: 'I lost six men.' He swerved abruptly on Alan, and, imploring, almost shouted: 'For Christ's sake. I lost six *men*. I lost...'

Alan's skin contracted; he was cold round his heart, and desolate and congealed with embarrassment. He had nothing to say.

In front of him, Holl was righting slowly, passing a forearm slowly to and fro across his face, and then rebuckling his webbing. He said: 'I must go and see to the lads.' His voice was almost normal again. He went off to see his men. It was quite dark now.

In the darkness, Alan too looked to his men; he was in charge of a section of the perimeter. He went, whispering, from point to point; the rough Indian voices answered him, whispering. Like dogs, the whispering voices returned to him, their keeper. He sat, with a rubber ground-sheet round him, his back against a tree. He thought of six men lost, and there was a hole in his mind for them. How many men would he lose, tomorrow, tonight even? He would tell them to go forward, to be killed. He sat on in the unending encompassing darkness, his thoughts returning again and again, sickly, to the bottomless gap that he could not bridge.

A voice hissing in his ear roused him almost into panic.

But it was only Sundar Singh, bearing a tin mug of tepid tea, and timorously proud of himself. It seemed a little lighter; the moon had risen above the trees, and Sundar's teeth were visible.

'Where on earth did you get that from?' It was warmer than it had seemed at first, almost solid, a rich confection of *ghi*, sugar, condensed milk and tea leaves. He sucked it down, and, revived, gave back the mug to Sundar Singh. Their hands touched, and a sudden warmth of gratitude flooded into Alan. Then he was ashamed.

'I found it,' Sundar Singh was saying. Then a note of almost auntly concern crept into his voice, and he told Alan reproachfully that his bivouac was waiting ready for him; his kit was arranged thus and thus.

The sahib should go there and get some sleep.

Then, across his whispering voice, the night cracked like a huge whip. Convulsive on his feet, revolver in hand, Alan peered helplessly to and fro at the viscous dusk. There were no more shots, but an agitation of voices away on his right; hurriedly he made his way towards it, to find a havildar berating a sepoy who had loosed off. He swore he had seen a man creeping up towards them through the young rubber beyond their lines. 'There, there!' he insisted with one hand flung out. 'Ssh!' ordered the havildar. 'But *there*!' cried the sepoy suddenly, almost screaming, and they all realised that a figure was staggering towards them.

Alan raised his revolver, and men surged about him in confusion. But then – 'Don't fire!' he cried. 'Hold it!' A moment later the man reeled into his arms and collapsed, sobbing, and a moment after that, in a tornado of hissing oaths, the adjutant arrived from behind.

Dragging the man into the shelter of the rubber, they stopped. The adjutant shone a shielded torch, and swore violently. 'Stretcher-bearers! Get back, you! Get *back*!' But the knot of sepoys pressed tighter in appalled fascination; their voices sharp and yapping.

'It is Anant Ram!'

'Anant Ram.'

'Shot.'

'His hands!'

'*Ayee*, his hands, his hands!'

'His head!'

'Anant Ram!'

The man lay forward across the lap of one of his comrades; in the spot of the torch his hands, bound behind his back, jerked grotesquely, feebly, fish-shaped. The light shifted up his body, up the reddened shirt. He was bareheaded, and the right-hand side of his head at the back was a shining crimson mess of blood and hair.

'Tied him up and shot from behind,' said the adjutant, his voice snarling yet thoughtfully astonished. 'Get his hands free. Easy now, *easy*!'

It was not easy, because the wrists were lashed with telephone wire, and the stretcher party arrived before they were freed. The man seemed to have fainted; they laid him face down on the stretcher and moved off towards the casualty station.

'O.K., Alan,' said the adjutant. 'But just rub into your blokes that the next man who looses off without an order will get a drumhead court-martial.'

Later that night, Alan sat again under his tree. In the meantime, though there had been no further alarms, Anant Ram had recovered enough to tell. Two men had been killed outright in Holl's first charge; four had then got detached, and had been captured by the slippery enemy. After a time the Japanese had tied their hands behind their backs, knelt them down, and shot them in the head from behind; only him had they shot not very thoroughly. They did not take prisoners.

The night had congealed now in a thick greyish mist that hung like damp gauze curtains amongst the tree trunks: through it came the throb of frogs, and the moan and sharp stinging dive of mosquitoes. Alan was engaged in a cold, concentrated battle with sickness; he could not be sick in hearing of his troops, but he could not rid his mind of the clotted mess that had been Anant Ram's head. The surges of nausea alternated with rages of impotent anger; he wanted to stamp and rage, to loose off machine-gun fire, but he was also, all the time, cold with a cold that seemed to move outwards from his stomach in a creeping ague. It took him a long time to realise that this was not the cold of the damp night, but of fear; when he did realise it at last, he was startled and then aloofly amused, and greeted his fear with something like relief, but courteously, as if raising a hat, and suddenly was relaxed.

When he next found himself thinking, he had been asleep, and was very stiff and numbed. He roused himself; it was two-thirty. He made a tour of his forward posts; everything was in order. He whispered for a little with a jemadar, and returned to his tree. This time he lay flat. He slept after a fashion; his mind, while never losing consciousness of its heavy body, lumped on the earth yet with ears turned on like microphones, escaped into a series of fragmentary dreams, landscapes, rooms and corridors, all lit impartially by a hard unshadowy light, and all empty yet informed by the lingering farewell of somebody whom he was urgently seeking. At last he was in a room he knew, his parents' sitting room, and though this too was empty there hung in it, like cigarette smoke in sunshine, George's phrase: *personal survival before death* – but the sound was the memory of Lettice's voice, and then for a second, he seemed to catch sight of her at last. She was in full evening dress, a gown of silver floating down the path outside the window, but as he shouted despairingly he felt the glass between them cutting off his words and there was silence again as he saw her absorbed in rank upon rank of marching men in black evening dress. He groaned; and a finger nudged him from behind with laughter, and he turned, wild and silly with hope.

It was Sundar Singh again, his finger poking decorously at Alan's shoulder. Alan was to report at once to the C.O. Dazed, he got up, and went, uncertainly, fending off trees, towards Battalion H.Q. The air was whitening, milky yet sharp. Men were stirring from the ground.

Scrapings was squatting on an ammunition box, drinking tea, unshaven and grey. 'Ah, Mart. I'm sending you down to contact the Australian battalion.' He was to move in one of the three armoured cars that had arrived the previous evening. 'Better take an orderly; there won't be room for more, with Sam and his orderly.'

'Holl!' Alan was shocked. Not with Holl.

'Holl will go on to Brigade if all is well. I want him to report personally to the brigadier. I think he'll be able to get transport from the Australians down to Brigade, and you can come back in the car. My God, I'd give a million rupees to have the faintest idea what's going on round here; that bloody wireless truck seems to've packed up for good.' His eyes rested bleakly on Alan, whose responsibility the wireless truck (a Brigade concern) was not.

Half an hour later, in the dawn, Alan met Holl by the armoured car. Holl gave him an uninterested, grim nod. He had a tommy-gun, and Alan his .45; their two orderlies had rifles. The car was driven by its volunteer driver, a long thin ex-tin miner, fortyish, gangling and sounding idiotically cheerful. He apologised, saying they would not be very comfy, and laughed gaily. Holl climbed up into the gunner's bucket seat, and contact with the machine gun that was the car's armament seemed to arouse a spark of interest in him for a moment. Alan and the two orderlies squeezed in, the door clanged shut, and the car started.

The journey, taken in silence apart from the driver's low tuneless whistling, seemed to last for hours. Alan could see nothing except by craning his neck to squint through the driver's slit at the slowly moving metallic road edged with green. He was profoundly uneasy, and could feel the wooded landscape about him crawling intimately with enemy like lice in a shirt. But more than that, Holl' s presence afflicted him; his eyes came back again and again to the massive back a few inches from him, and each time he remembered fearfully the sight of Holl in the dusk the night before, broken, hiccupping with tearless sobs.

After perhaps half an hour, or less, they were challenged. The car stopped, and Holl emerged through the turret to hold a brief conversation with two morose Australians. The car moved on some hundred yards and stopped again.

'Wait here a second, Alan,' said Holl. 'They said their bloody H.Q. was somewhere round here, but it's as quiet as the grave. I'll just get our bearings and be back.' He got out, followed by his orderly. Alan uncoiled his cramped limbs thankfully, and squirmed up into the gunner's seat; the driver started an odd off-beat conversation about the virtues and failings of armoured cars. He sounded affectionate about them, though dwelling on their unsuitability for this sort of country. Holl seemed to be gone for a long time. Alan stared down the road, which ran straight ahead between rubber for about a hundred and fifty yards and then swung to the right; it was edged with thick low scrub, above which rose the trunks of the rubber trees. There was not a soul in sight; never had Alan seen so empty a road, and as Holl did not come back he began to feel there must be some mistake – they could not be in the middle of the Australian position.

The driver had lit a cigarette. '*Will* drop things from trees, the little baskets,' he was saying, with something of the vexed affection of an uncle for rowdy small nephews, when he suddenly stopped in mid-sentence. From forward there came the sound of fairly heavy firing – some machine gun, and something heavier than machine gun; it sounded queerly both near and far away, but was obviously getting nearer in a way that Alan could not explain to himself. No one in the car spoke for what seemed to Alan ages. Then the driver with a neat gesture flicked his cigarette out of the open turret, and listened for a bit with his head on one side, and one elbow resting easily on his controls. Then he reached up, clanged down the lid of the turret, and turned to Alan with a look of radiant, half-sly expectation, like a child coming into a party.

'Sounds like some fun going on up there, he said. 'Let's wander up and see if we can lend a hand, shall us?'

'*What*!' cried Alan, shocked rigid.

But the car was already moving. Too startled to think, uncertain of his own standing *vis-à-vis* this wild driver, he did the only thing possible, and looked to the machine gun. He had never got far enough up the queue at the Cadet College actually to fire one of these, but he knew about it in theory, and had stripped them before now. The grips were reassuringly solid. He gripped them. The gun moved easily; a belt of ammunition was engaged. He found the safety catch, and was just adjusting himself to the sights, when he realised that the firing had almost stopped ahead. But there was another noise to which it had given place; a rumbling, lumbering noise, terribly ominous, though he could not for a second think what it was. Then he heard the driver give a strange throttled shout, and glancing down, saw him engaged in convulsive battle with hands and feet on all controls at once. Alan shouted too, in a panic of bewilderment, and looking up to the road again was in time to see a tank moving round the bend towards him. His eyes studied, amidst a complete capsizal of his mind, the fact that it was a tank, that it was flying a little pennant, white with a splash of orange, that it had a waddling, immensely ponderous gait; that it had two guns, one in the turret that was swinging to the car like a gross compass needle to a magnet. His back was cowering against the backless bucket seat, his feet thrusting as if to push the car back, and then the car was indeed going backwards, but slowly, in snail-slow reverse. Then suddenly his hands discovered the machine gun again, and he went into action just as the tank's turret gun focused on him. Throbbing with the staccato clangour of the gun, his mouth opened, groaning despairingly. His eyes were swamped with sweat, and then clenched shut against the impact of the shell that must come. The movement of the car beneath him slewed sideways, and almost simultaneously a huge buffet smacked it flat.

Yet not flat. Flung up, crashed against steel, tossed down and across, half-stunned, with his head booming and splitting, Alan found himself still nevertheless alive, and at rest, lying on his side looking across the road into bright sunlit green bushes. He was still inside the car; its off wheel had gone into the roadside ditch, just before the tank fired, and the shell had only caught a glancing blow. Alan was looking out through the turret lid which had flown open; the car was on its side. Across his vision churned grey caterpillar tracks, three feet away, and then again, and again. Inside the car, Alan lay waiting for the explosion that would finish it; he lay unmoving, tensed rigid against the blow that must come, yet passive in compliance. But the fourth tank had stopped in the midst of a wild crashing noise, and every gun on earth seemed to be firing. The caterpillar tracks moved, and then stopped again. In front of Alan's eyes was now the rear of the tank; two wicker cages were attached to it and in them were some cowering hens. They had a stupid but reptilian look, as though the tank had given birth. One of them winked and in Alan's head, as if in a hollow scooped out of the bedlam of battle, he heard an isolated cluck. Then one of them fluttered, and as if in sympathy his own body came to, and his mind started to stutter that this was no place for hens. But again, as if in that hollow within his head, he heard the voices of men talking in a strange tongue. They were shouting inside the tank not more than five feet from his head. He noted this; it did not seem to make sense. He found he could move a little, and looked round inside the car. The volunteer driver was apparently alive, but curiously involved with the controls, his hands shielding his face. Twisting, Alan discovered, behind him, rolled in a small ball, Sundar Singh, his face a purplish grey but his eyes, dismayed and popping, looking into Alan's a foot away. His face suddenly brought back to Alan that he, Alan, was in command in this armoured car. He gave Sundar a resolute ghastly grin, and, knowing at last where he was, turned back to his viewpoint of the chickens. Here were tanks; to deal with tanks, you fire into their tracks. Preferably of course with an anti-tank gun or rifle; however, he worked his .45 free of its holster, shoved himself up on to one elbow, and fired thoughtfully and dutifully into the near track of the tank. He could not hear his shot but knew he had fired because of the recoil. He fired again and then again. The tank looked exactly the same, until suddenly it started to back away. He caught it again with a shot in the front of the track before it vanished. Then the second tank appeared, also backing past. He fired his last two shots into that, and then had to reload. His fingers were maddeningly clumsy, but he felt busy, unafraid and curiously content. He glanced over his shoulder at Sundar Singh before taking up his firing position again. Sundar looked much the same. Alan grinned. 'O.K.,' he said. '*Thik hai*, Sundar *ji*. We'll be all right.'

He waited now for the other two tanks to come past, but no more appeared. Then he began to get worried; he had not put these tanks out of action, and they must be swivelling to concentrate all guns on him, who, as far as he knew, in spite of all the noise of hell outside, was the only one on his side fighting this battle. The momentary sense of important invulnerability that had possessed him when he discovered that he was still alive began to drain away, and suddenly the prostrate car was a rat-trap, with them helpless inside awaiting the *coup de grâce*. The fury of gunfire continued outside, and he realised that he had no idea what was happening out there, and that he could do nothing. It did not make sense; what were the tanks doing, where was all the firing coming from?

Then, following a tremendous crescendo of noise, that forced him flat, his hands over his head, there welled out a sound unlike anything he had ever heard, a tortured entwining screaming of voices animal rather than human, as though throats of flesh were tearing like canvas. Alan clutched his head; it felt as though nothing could survive the agony of that cry. Long after it had died and drowned in the battering gunfire he lay still, as if paralysed.

He was aroused by the driver, who squirmed across him towards the turret opening and lay stuck for a moment heavily on top of him. Sheer necessity to breathe roused Alan from his coma.

The driver squinted down at him. He was shouting.

Alan made out that the driver was going to make a break for it, and almost before he had taken this in, the driver's boot caught him a sharp blow on the temple as he kicked clear of the car. Blinking, Alan saw him scud across the road and dive headlong into the scrub on the far side. Still he took some time to grasp the idea that it was possible to leave the car. When this had sunk in, he adjusted his body, as if by remote control, to its implications, wriggling forward so that he could launch himself out. He looked back to see what his orderly was doing; rolled even tighter now, like a dormouse hibernating, Sundar had almost vanished except for a gleam of watery despairing eyes. Alan shouted at him, and made encouraging gestures with one hand and forward motions with his head. Then, taking a deep breath, he ejected himself on to the road, which proved enormously open, murderous, spitting and clanging with gunfire, and apparently half a mile wide. The brushwood on the far side took him with a clutch of whipping twigs, and he was flat, his mouth loving the earth, his hands scrabbling. The breath came out of him in a harsh grunt. Over him the air crackled and spluttered like a gigantic frying pan. A large clumsy missile burst through the undergrowth, and landed a yard away, a little above Alan, who bit farther into the grit, and shut himself against an explosion which never came. Instead, with a high, whistling moan, Sundar's voice. Alan turned his head, his eyes smarting with dust, and found Sundar's face, radiant with emotion, his eyes swivelling, his mouth open and crying '*Ayee*, *ayee*!'

'*Ssh*!' Alan said fatuously and smugly, and then cowered again, as the air burst yet more fiercely above them. Then it seemed as though someone were calling him, but from a hidden place like a voice calling through fog; lifting his head he turned this way and that, and saw that a movement above him, some twenty feet away, was an arm gesturing; then into the arm rose Holl's body, and Holl came slithering down towards him, heaved him on all fours and sent him, with a great slap on the buttocks, staggering up the bank, where he fell into a slit trench almost on top of a bronzed fair-headed boy who was stripped to the waist.

'*Wow*!' said the boy, and then something that Alan could not catch. Panting for breath, he squatted at the bottom of the trench. He could see up the boy's back to a blue sky shredded by green leaves, and he saw the angle of the boy's right elbow as it jerked, and the movement back and forward as he worked his rifle bolt. Then Sundar, closely followed by Holl, fell heavily on top of him. Eventually Holl's face sorted itself out an inch or so from his. It was fixed in a grinning snarl, and then its lower jaw started to wag up and down. '*By God!*' Holl was shouting – almost screaming – '*By God!*' – over and over again as though he had suffered a glory of revelation.

The young Australian soldier turned for a second to stoop for his helmet; he cocked it rakishly on one side of his head, and braced himself against the walls of the weapon pit to fire again. But then he lowered his rifle, and beckoned the others to stand up and look.

With infinite caution Alan surfaced, and at once ducked involuntarily, for he was looking at an angle down the road at four tanks less than fifty yards away. When he came up again, he saw that the road behind them was blocked by an enormous tree felled across it; from one of the tanks rose a sluggish dense black smoke, and two of the others showed no sign of life. Only the fourth, as he watched, jerked as one of its guns fired with a puff of whitish smoke up the road, away from them. Then he saw what the others were looking at – a single khaki-clad figure with a tin hat garlanded with green leaves, that dodged neatly out from the edge of the road, vanished in the smoke of the burning tank, and reappeared, almost shimmying, beyond; for a moment it poised with one arm upraised, in a balanced perilous stillness that brought Alan to his toes, his scalp prickling – then, with a spring, the man's body bounded on and off the still-active tank, one hand slapping it with a derisive gesture, as if across the face. The man slid back and sideways to the shelter of the road-side scrub, seeming impossibly vulnerable, and Alan felt something inside stretching in sympathy almost to breaking point; but the attacker reached shelter, and Alan saw that the tank now was gushing with black smoke, while about it welled out that terrible cry that he had heard before from inside the car, and that he now knew was the agony of men burning alive. Its vibration penetrated his whole body as though it were porous; he shook with it until he all but shattered like a glass. Gradually it died, fading, leaving the air emptied and faint. Alan found his hands were clutching his elbows, his nails sharp in his flesh, but a new noise, braying harsh and merciless in triumph, flared up amongst the trees, and everywhere men resurrected from the earth, cheering, bawling, waving. At his side Holl was shouting like a madman, his mouth a roaring hole, his eyes shining inane and empty. The Australian at his side too stood clutching his rifle to his sweat-gleaming body, his face visionary as if with a vanishing dream, his mouth moving softly in prayer. 'Whacko, whacko!' he said. 'Oh, Ginger! Oh, the bleeding sods! Ah, *whacko*, Ginger!'

In the middle of this, unannounced, a huge flatulent bang. Alan ducked. When he peered up again, the ground had emptied of men. The dream had passed from the Australian's face, which now looked younger than ever but tired and sulky; he was saying in a hard and regretful voice: 'Mortars again. Bloody mortars.'

Alan stared at him, and then at Holl. He did not understand. 'I don't understand,' he said. Something of tremendous importance had happened, and he could not grasp it. A second breathy bang, unasked as a balloon bursting at a supper party, sent him lower still in the slit-trench. 'I don't understand. What's happened?'

Holl's face turned to him. Holl's eyes recognised him, and explored him in astonishment that gave way to delight. Holl's hand came out and held his wrist, tight and holding down. 'Christ, sonny, I thought you were a goner. By God, I *knew* you were a goner.'

'But what's happening?'

Gradually, through the noise above, Alan began to get his bearings. Their armoured car had passed on the road two positions of anti-tank guns, so well camouflaged that they had not noticed them even from behind; their car had then stopped right in the middle of the Australians' carefully prepared tank-trap, and there Holl had got out. When the tanks appeared, one tree was felled neatly between the first two tanks while the guns in the rear simultaneously knocked them out with direct hits. Some hundred yards forward, at the same moment, behind the rear four tanks, another tree had crashed down, and the forward guns had disposed of two directly, and hamstrung the third, while the fourth was shielded by the other three, It was this fourth tank that the redoubtable shimmying Ginger had just annihilated with a Molotov cocktail.

Hunched in the bottom of the slit-trench, Alan considered this news, slowly digesting it. Six out of six of those armoured juggernauts had been wiped out. It occurred to him that he too, with his tiny pistol, had fought them, and had not been vanquished. He began to glow; he bubbled with victory. The air had grown quieter again. Holl and the Australian were looking out over the top; their legs stood about him, dirty and sturdy. Crouched opposite him, knees touching his, was Sundar Singh, his eyes searching Alan's for explanation. Alan offered him a stern, confident smile as explanation and gave him a thumbs-up, nodding with authority. Sundar smiled back, but jerkily, uneasily. Still glowing, Alan stood up, stretching. About them stood the grey-green trunks flecked with sunlight. It was almost quiet where they were, though heavy automatic fire was continuous from forward. Holl was explaining warmly to the Australian that if in the past he had let slip certain comments on Australia and Australians that might not have been entirely favourable, he had done so not from malice but out of sheer ignorance, for it was now clear to him that Australians were the finest fighting troops in the world. The Australian took this almost bashfully; he said he knew they had funny accents and that put off a lot of people from Home.

A light wind moved in Alan's hair, and he realised that he had lost his turban in the car. 'To hell with it,' he thought with joy. He pushed his webbing straight, squared his shoulders, took a deep breath, and said: 'Well, we'd better be getting along to Brigade, Sam. Have to foot it, though. Poor old car's broken.' He laughed riotously. 'Or do I stay here? Did you locate their H. Q.?'

Holl turned to look at him, and was silent with astonishment for a moment. Then the Australian laughed on a mocking note, and Alan found himself blushing, bewildered again.

'You stay here, sonny,' said Holl. 'Like the rest of us. They're all round us.'

Alan blinked. 'Who's all round us?'

Holl stared harder. 'Dancing girls,' he said. 'Lovely dancing girls, crying come and get it.'

'Oh,' Alan sat down again. He felt idiotic; the war was not over, and neither he nor the Australians had yet won it.

'They say,' said Holl, biting at his lips, 'that the Japs have got a whole division on this road.'

The Australian nodded. 'Imperial Chrysanthemums, or some such fairies. Their crack troops. But we'll give 'em crack.' The sister

Australian battalion was astride the road four miles in the rear, and a British brigade was rumoured to be coming up behind them. 'And then there's your boys,' said the Australian. 'Or what's left of them. How did you manage to get out of Muar yesterday? I heard every white officer in that battalion was dead.'

Holl was explaining that he and Alan had not come from that battalion. The Australian did not know much about it, except that the battalion seemed to have faded in about an hour. 'Busy little runners; nimble on their toes,' he said. 'Poor little sods; they were pretty new, though, weren't they? Bloody criminal, shoving 'em up in front like that.'

Holl's face had gone bleak. He stared angrily at the Australian, but said nothing. Alan felt weak on his legs; and sank to the bottom of the trench again. He tried to grapple with the idea of a whole battalion vanished, and a confused, impotent anger filled his eyes with tears. It was all so unfair. What could two Australian battalions and half an Indian brigade, without aeroplanes, tanks or even artillery support, do against a fully equipped division? He swore fiercely under his breath. Seeing Sundar's face, anxious still and open as a question mark, he shut his eyes and turned his head away. He could not think at all. Reopening his eyes, he saw a large red ant that walked up the duller red earth of the trench wall; weaving briskly, it went up as though gravity meant nothing to it, until it met a projecting stone; after some feinting about this, it fell abruptly on to Alan's bare knee. He looked at it as it twisted its head to and fro, lost for the moment. He had fellow-feeling for the ant. With a sharp pinging sting the ant bit him; with a sharper slap he killed it.

'Christ!' he said, loudly. 'Ants!' He looked fixedly at Sundar Singh, almost accusingly. Sundar Singh looked miserable, but especially stupid. Blind anger swept Alan's mind; he stood up. 'Let's go,' he said to Holl.

'Go?' Holl broke off his questioning of the Australian.

'Better locate their H.Q.' Alan spoke firmly and masterfully. 'Find out what's going on. We've got to get back somehow.' He felt as he had often felt in a game of rugger, fighting on his own line; a blind fury to shut his eyes and get his head down and throw the opponents backward, but he was surprised all the same when Holl agreed. They got directions from the Australian and climbed out. Holl's orderly, looking rather sheepish and unhappy, joined them from another slit-trench nearby. The firing forward was still intense but seemed to have slackened a little and to be fairly distant. They set off parallel with the road, in single file, Holl leading. They passed scattered groups of Australians; they passed an improbable photographer skipping and crouching to get shots of the tanks. Then Alan stopped dead; ten yards from the tanks, two Japanese lay at the side of the road: one on his back, his feet wide, while the second man's close-cropped head rested on the other's stomach and seemed to be nuzzling into it. They were dressed in dirty-looking breeches and shirts, with ragged puttees. Alan looked at them, and then away; his mind rocked. Then his eyes dragged back to the two bodies, and searched them with a voracious curiosity; the litter of their heavy lolling deadness seemed almost his own. He could not move. He saw a group of Australians, who had been examining the tanks, turn to the bodies. With a delicate boot, one of them prised the upper half on its side; then, released, it fell back. Alan felt his own arm lift; then it fell back, and its weight seemed to leave a dark bruise that invaded his whole flesh.

At his side Holl was sucking at his teeth and working at his lips, and then growled: 'To think that *that*'s what's been pushing back trained British troops...' His head nodded with exasperation. Then he moved on.

Alan followed, stumbling. His feet were numb; his breath made a hissing, snarling noise.

All noise of battle seemed suddenly to be stilled.

All that day Holl and Alan stayed with the Australians, who were indeed cut off. Most of their effort was towards their rear – to clear the road and open it back to the supporting battalion behind. Apart from this they were concerned simply to hold their position, to survive beneath the ceaseless sniping and mortar fire, and to flush out odd enemy machine gun positions by surprise but strictly limited counter-attacks. Four times they were dive bombed.

With them Alan and Holl lodged comfortably, two officers each with only an orderly to command, feeling embarrassed and supernumerary as passengers. But as the day drew on their admiration for their hosts grew even higher, so coolly and methodically did they go about their business. And at last, just as dusk began to close, a wave of cheering flared from the rear of their perimeter, and down the road came the first convoy to get through that day. Men rose from the ground as they had that morning after the destruction of the tanks, and again that harsh unhuman roar swept the troops. Tin hats waved; rifles flourished; men rushed the vehicles as though they were floats in a flower carnival, and Alan saw that an elderly sergeant who stood close by him was fiercely weeping.

The battle seemed to be subsiding, and by the time it was dark the lack of noise was almost disturbing. An order had come through, by some mystic means via Brigade and wireless, that Holl and Alan were to proceed back if possible at first light next morning across country to their own unit. Holl had said little all day; the news of the disaster of their sister battalion in Muar had temporarily shocked him out of confidence. Only with the reopening of the road in the evening did he seem to recover; as the shouting died, he turned to Alan, and announced with enthusiasm that the first thing he was going to do when peace was signed was to emigrate down under. Then he paused, and seemed wary. 'But,' he said, 'if the Aussies can do this, so can our *jawans*. We just hold 'em together, see, and keep them on the attack; as soon as they've got their wind they'll go through the little yellow runts split-arse like a knife through butter.'

Morale was good; there was even talk of a counter-attack supported by heavy reinforcements coming up from the south-east, to retake the town. Alan and Holl settled for the night, and Alan slept on the ground almost as soon as he stretched out, until about ten, when the sound of firing fairly close aroused him. Soon after word passed that snipers were infiltrating, and soon after that the Japanese began to put down a few rounds of mortar fire every few minutes indiscriminately around the Australian position. No one got much sleep until a little before dawn, when the noise all stopped abruptly. Alan took advantage to move over to a trench that served as latrine a little distance away.

and sat, feeling sleepy and foolish, but also curiously soothed by the fact that his bowels were working with regularity. He thought almost aloud that life goes on, and simultaneously it occurred to him that it would be foolish to be sniped in a latrine. He shrank down, clasping across his knees the rifle that he had borrowed off the Australians.

As he stood up, he heard a shot. There was a pause, and he stood alert. Then the trees crackled all over the place with firing as if in a running breeze, very alarmingly, as this was near the centre of the Australians' position and nowhere in sight even of the perimeter. He threw himself flat at the foot of a tree, feeling hugely exposed and ridiculously conscious that his fly was not buttoned. Groaning, he pushed his rifle forward; the barrel slid up over the fork of a branch of a small bush; thus it was handily supported but Alan did not know if it was pointing in the right direction or if there was indeed any right direction. It was light enough to see a little way, but he could see nothing. Immediately above him the air clenched and cracked, and he contracted. The firing went, round and about, sporadic, disconnected, aimless, until after a little he was used to it and thought that he could not stay there all day; he must bolt for his trench. He raised his head, with infinite caution. As he did so, he glimpsed, or thought he glimpsed, a flash on his foresight, as though the little knob there had sparked with lightning. Still, as if frozen, he was looking up along his barrel through the murky aisle of rubber trees, seeing, unbelieving, something that moved in the fork of a branch of one of them forty yards away. A terrible shiver moved outwards from his stomach; he thought feverishly that he would never steady his hands in time, but the butt of his rifle came smooth and cold and calm against his cheek, and suddenly his elbow was as firm as a rock, the safety catch moved, his finger closed with love upon the trigger. Again he saw the movement, his eyes straining; the fork of the branch slid into line – with his foresight and the shoulders of his backsight, and his finger squeezed.

The noise was appalling. And his eyes had shut as he fired; he was flattening blindly as a mole against the resisting earth. When the hiatus was over his first thought was that he had probably made a fool of himself and shot at an Australian. He raised his head in horror, in time to see the bundle in the fork of the tree articulate itself into a man, hanging for a moment head down by a foot trapped in the branch, and then fall with an audible thud to the ground. Stooping and shaking, Alan sped to the trench that he shared with Holl and their orderlies, and fell in, babbling in a whisper that he had shot a man.

'That was *you*?' said Holl.

'Is it a Jap?'

'You shockin' little poacher,' said Holl. 'I'd been waiting for him to move for five minutes – he was covered by the tree trunk, and I was just waiting...'

'Oh Christ!' said Alan, down a long expulsive sigh. 'I didn't know. I thought it might be an Australian.'

'Bloody idiot,' said Holl, referring not to Alan but to the sniper. 'Suicide wallahs. They said they worked like that and I didn't believe it. In broad daylight almost.' He turned to Alan. 'But that was nice shooting,' he said in admiration, with a certain tinge of incredulousness.

Through a profound relief that he had not done anything criminal, the incredulousness reached Alan, and all other feeling was eaten up in a brash bombast of pride. 'I shot him,' he announced quietly, and snapped his bolt back and forward, ejecting the spent cartridge.

Holl was grinning at him, and explaining to the orderlies that Mart sahib had shot a Japanese. The orderlies grinned too with a suppressed fervour, congratulating him, and peering eagerly over the top for enemies to shoot for themselves. But Alan was struck by a new emotion, hearing his own words repeating over and over in his head: *I shot him*. He, too, looked out and over to where the man had fallen, only to see a stretcher party moving in a hurried shuffle already on their way back, the laden stretcher jogging lumpily to their step. One of the stretcher party called across to them – '*One less*' – and gestured gaily with his thumb down. Alan felt an almost irresistible urge to go over and look at the man whom he had killed. But he stayed where he was, tracing doodles in the dust, and staring inanely through the lightening trees. It was almost broad daylight now, but there was no more firing; it had all ceased after the explosion of his own shot. Twenty yards away an Australian was sitting fully exposed on the edge of a slit-trench, yawning, and cleaning his rifle. Everywhere people were moving. In his mind Alan muddled about with the fact that he had killed a man. The light had come so swiftly that the shooting seemed like a dream, and like a dream to have lost its inner coherence and significance as the dreamer waked. He wondered, in duty to a humane education, whom he had killed; he thought that now he'd done it, now he'd shot down the whole set of pacifist principles in which till now he had framed his hope. He thought for the hundred thousandth time since he had joined the Army that he must arrive at new principles to replace those that he had denied, but his mind said only with a cold already forgetting glee – *Now you've done it*! He felt a mild physical urge to do some more, but it was really nothing important (once that first expansive pride had ebbed). He had squeezed a trigger and a thing had fallen obediently off a tree like a coconut. There wasn't even any prize; no coconut to keep. It was like scoring one's first try at rugger. And suddenly he diagnosed what he was really feeling: a mean resentment, for he had been slightly cheated.

Holl had been out of the trench and was now back and talking to Alan. Alan attended to Holl, who was saying the Red Caps would come and get him.

Alarm and guilt lifted Alan's voice to a squeak. 'But I didn't do anything.'

'Indecent exposure, sonny. Latch up your trousers.'

Alan was fumbling foolishly with his buttons when the Australian major appeared with a section of his men; he was lending them for escort for the cross-country trek back to the Indian battalion. 'All quiet so far,' said the major. We thought there'd be a big attack at dawn, but nothing yet, not a Nip in sight; too bloody quiet for my liking. One of our patrol's just come in from the north along the way you'll be going out, and they haven't seen a thing. But I should move now; yesterday was just kidding about with a soft ball compared with what we'll get today.'

He escorted them to the northern edge of the perimeter, and wished them luck. They went in a V formation, starting out through young rubber, marching north-west by compass. They trod lightly with furtive haste, and not till they had gone some two miles, including a narrow path through a strip of jungle, did they move with any confidence. After a little more than an hour they skirted a planter's bungalow, empty, with two shutters hanging loose on the veranda and a trail of battered and broken objects – chairs, frying pans, bedding, boxes – littered from the front door in the bright sun. Holl stopped. He asked the Australian corporal if he'd have any objection if they had a look for some breakfast in the bungalow.

The corporal said he could spare five minutes.

'Right!' said Holl to Alan. 'Just case that joint. We've got you covered. And bring back anything alive that's edible. I'm hungry.'

Alan went in very gingerly. Looters had already dealt with the house, violently if not thoroughly. The living room had been a place of some luxury, but the heart had been torn out of it; ripped chairs showed their entrails, and smashed pictures, cushions, glasses and capsized tables strewed the floor. The room held a close, wounded silence, and Alan found himself tiptoeing into the kitchen. This had been gutted, but, high up on a shelf, he found some biscuits and some tins of sardines, and then, tilted against the wall under a table, an open but almost full bottle of vermouth. With this loot he emerged into the hot sun of the clearing. The Australians had already breakfasted, and the two orderlies would only eat biscuits. For a few brief minutes Alan sat alongside Holl on a log, eating sardines and biscuits and drinking Italian vermouth and water. It was a still and beautiful morning; over the roof of the bungalow palm trees drooped elegant shining-green heads, and the air smelled crisp and astringent though already hot. They ate hurriedly, and in silence. Alan's eyes were fixed on the palm trees cut so still on the blue sky; he had a curious sensation that everywhere, except where he was, was holiday. Palms were the south of France, the blue sea wearing the long sand like a scarf, and an odour of sun oil on flesh cooking for love. But he looked at Holl, and Holl was not holiday, in his sweat-stained khaki shirt and shorts, with the stubble of a day's beard on his hardened face. Alan shut his eyes. *Un arbre*, said his mind, giddy, *berce sa palme. Pardessus le toit, si bleu, si calme*. The vermouth tasted bitter-sweet, sickening, its sweetness the sweetness of Communion wine. He remembered in a flash the rite of Confirmation, the bishop's hand upon his unoiled hair, the bishop's face shining with surely antiseptic soap. *La paisible rumeur de la ville*, said his mind, dismissing the vision. A warm tide of lassitude rose in his head, sealing his eyelids, stupefying. With a jerk, he came to; he had been asleep. Holl had paused with the bottle on its way to his lips, and was listening. From the south came a heavy rumble.

'They've started,' said Holl, putting the bottle down. 'We must move.' But he paused again a moment, looking hard at Alan. 'This is it,' he said. 'The battalion will be in action today. I never thought it would be like this, but this is it, and by God I'm going to drive our boys through those bastards if I have to whip them.'

'Yes,' said Alan, fully awake now. He stood up, and took the bottle and a last swig neat. It seemed to taste like blood and gall drenched in sugar, and he spat. As he did so he remembered again the obscene blood-sweetness of Communion wine, and shivered.

'Christ,' he said, not swearing but as if tentatively interrogative. But Holl was moving already; the Australians were moving, heavy but lithe and purposeful, guns at the ready. Alan hurried to get into place. Pistol in hand, he trod delicately and with a chill determination. I killed a man, said his mind.

SIX

HOLL AND ALAN reached their own troops without incident, and found them formed up ready to move. A messenger had come through across country from Brigade, and their orders were to close on Brigade Headquarters, passing through the Australian positions on their way. They were to march across country, taking with them anti-tank rifles, bren guns and 2-inch mortars; the transport was to proceed on its own down the side road that connected them with the main road astride which were the two Australian battalions; if it could not get through it was to be destroyed and abandoned.

Holl, though now acting second-in-command in the absence of the major (who was believed to be with Brigade), took over his own company again. Alan was appointed to guide the battalion by the route that he and Holl had come that morning. He had barely time to locate his kit, already packed into a truck, and to change his heavy boots for gym shoes. Straightening up, he looked at his valise and suitcase sadly, and, realising he might well never see them again, pulled out from them Lettice's letters. He pushed these in his ammunition pouches and set off for the head of the column; on his way he passed the adjutant, who was rocking gently on his heels and whistling softly. He had a strange air of one embarrassed and also of hiding something. As he passed, Alan glimpsed, beyond the adjutant, Scrapings on his knees in the privacy of a little shelter formed by some bushes. It took Alan a few moments, as he went on, to realise that Scrapings was in prayer, and the realisation embarrassed him too and also made him very uneasy.

They marched swiftly and without meeting any opposition, and by one o clock Alan was back almost to where he had spent the night within the Australian perimeter, in the hot and sticky midday silence of the battle wood. The Australian troops he spoke to seemed jumpy if stoical. They had repelled two biggish attacks that morning, both from their front; a small convoy had come through early that morning from their supporting battalion, but nothing since, and a dive bomber had got their wireless truck and a lot of their ammunition in the first of the two attacks. The Australians said again that they did not like this quiet.

Scrapings was conferring with the Australian C.O. When he returned he called his Order group, and gave his directions calmly, clearly and without emotion. In short, the battalion was to proceed down the road until they reached the rear Australian battalion. The officers were squatting about him in a semicircle on the edge of the Australian perimeter. Beyond them the rubber ceased, and an area of low bush, saturated with sunshine, sloped down to an expanse some three hundred yards wide of brilliant green rice paddy fields, thigh-deep in water. Across these ran a small causeway, carrying the road through to the thickly wooded rise beyond, where it entered a cutting.

The battalion would march in order of companies; H.Q. Company sandwiched between the four fighting companies.

Scrapings said that the road had been known to be free of enemy at dawn, but on the other hand the enemy had been on it in some strength the day before, and that the troops must be ready to engage at any moment. Alan, opposite Scrapings, looked out over his shoulder across the vivid rice fields at the wood beyond; as Scrapings' voice continued terse but level, Alan's skin began to contract and shiver in the small of his back, and a cold sweat to run from his armpits. Scrapings' voice went on, but buzzing fitfully now in Alan's ears and his eyes searched with an appalled certainty the road down which they would have to march, and the jungle that beset it. Instead of Scrapings' voice he heard Holl's as it had said, almost primly, earlier that morning: *suicide wallahs... I didn't believe it...* His eyes dragged from the heavy lurking green of the jungle, and stopped on Holl's face. Holl was listening avidly to Scrapings. Alan thought in panic that he, too, must listen to Scrapings. He concentrated, but his eyes were still on Holl, and Holl's eyes were slanted straining under his lids like the eyes of a man who knows the threat behind him. Alan knew that Holl knew as well as he that the Japanese were thick as the trees on the ground through which they had to pass.

Ten minutes later the march began. A Company led off, with Harold Hockey's short stout figure, chest thrown splendidly out, revolver in hand, in front of his men. With rifles at the trail, they moved unchallenged out into the glare of the sun, on to the causeway, where suddenly they looked pathetically small and vulnerable, and over and up into the cutting. B Company followed, and hard behind them Battalion Headquarters, the colonel, the adjutant and their runners, and then the subadar-major, in command of Headquarters Company. As Headquarters Company moved out, fairly heavy small arms fire sounded from down the road. Alan was up with his men on the road still in the shelter of the rubber; he heard the outbreak of firing just as he was passing Holl, who was squatting in a ditch by the road; for a moment their eyes locked. Holl's irises seemed to have dilated, hugely grey and cold, with a staring fixity that riveted Alan. He saw Holl's tongue pass swiftly over his lips, and then Holl raised his right hand with the revolver in it – a gesture that seemed simply one of dismissal.

Stumbling, Alan hurried on, and as he came out of the shade the sun hit him like a spotlight and he was out there dazzled and naked, walking into the sound of the firing. His men went plodding on iron heels with a small disjointed rhythm down the open road to the causeway. The noise seemed a half-mile or more in front, but the sweat started to run down into Alan's eyes, to sear under his webbing and in his crotch. On the causeway he found himself walking with delicate dizziness as on a tightrope. Then they were over the cause way, and into the cutting whose walls, seeming almost vertical, were soon shoulder-high, then high above their heads. In front of them the turbaned figures plodded on round the bend a hundred and fifty yards away; behind them more troops streamed continuously from the rubber. The din in front was now noticeably louder, but Alan seemed to move in his own silence towards it, and he could hear the noise of his men's boots accumulating like the slow rumour of scree that foretells avalanche. It was the cessation of this small noise that announced to him their own immediate ambush rather than the first shot, the lash of which seemed to come after the men had stopped in their tracks.

As Alan stood motionless, a second shot lifted his hair with its wind, and without further warning the teeming silence of the brooding jungle on each side of them burst into explosion. The long trail of men wavered, then some dived for the foot-deep, foot-wide gutter at the side of the road; others raised their rifles and started to fire, standing where they had stopped; others tried to scrabble up the steep sides of the cutting. Alan screamed, almost falsetto, at his men, and they tumbled towards the hopelessly inadequate gutter. Alan was flat there too, searching the top of the bank on the other side for a target, but finding nothing. The fire seemed to be coming out of unmanned trees. Farther up, he could hear mortar shells bursting now, but, glancing down, found Sundar Singh flat at his side probing the air in search of a quarry with his rifle barrel, like a dog pointing. His presence was oddly reassuring, and Alan knelt up, encouraged and astonished that he had not been hit, to try to see what was happening. Although a bullet passing with a vicious crack and stamp into the bank behind him made him duck, he realised that most of the shooting going on must be blind, and over their heads. He could see only a few casualties tumbled on the road; it was farther up and apparently just round the bend that the heavy stuff was going on. He took a deep breath, stood up, and waved his men on. It was just as they had started to move uncertainly up the road again that he saw movement too at the bend; but it was not a movement forward – the men were coming back. For a second he glimpsed a figure who seemed to be waving them back, but a mortar shell burst simultaneously in the road just short of the bend and another with a huge cloud of dust in the bank. The men were coming back at a run now, streaming past him as he stood. They ran with limbs fairly well composed as if in a middle-distance race but their heads down as if against rain; a few shouted or moaned unintelligibly as they ran. Helpless, he stood, as they pounded past. Then he started off against the stream, only to halt again at once. Snarling, he raised his revolver against one of the running men. The man gave him an apologetic, foolish and breathless smile, and pounded past. Alan lowered his gun. Then suddenly he found that he was all alone in the middle of the road, nothing, nobody except some inert figures, between him and the swirling dust at the bend a hundred yards away. Glancing this way and that, he found that Sundar was still flat in the gutter, his eyes watching Alan dismayed and uncomprehending, and Alan thought that Sundar must have been hit. As he turned towards him, something flicked his calf like a whiplash, stopping him. He saw that blood was running down his leg. He saw also Sundar rise and run, shouting. He looked at Sundar running in bewilderment; he looked at his leg. A terrible despair flooded him; he was hit, he was wounded, he would have to fall down in the road that was running with bullets like hail. He was still looking at his blood running down his leg when he found that his legs too were running, running under him, moving up and down, regular and mechanical and strong as pistons, as he fled back to the end of the cutting.

He threw himself down in the mud at the edge of the paddy, and found himself on his back. One of Holl's V.C.O.s was crouching over him. Alan looked at his face without hope. The man was shaking him by the shoulder; his face was grave and stern, his eyes dark and urgent over a neat moustache. Suddenly Alan turned on his face, convulsed by a shame so bitter and so selfish that his teeth grated and his nails dug into his hands.

A great hand gripped his shoulder and flung him face up. Holl stood over him, blacking out the sky, his eyes that had been so huge shrunk now to pin points, his revolver quivering in his hand. Alan looked with desire, with love, at the revolver. But Holl stooped again, to lift Alan to his knees.

'You're hit. Can you walk?'

Alan nodded, and could not stop nodding. He could not speak. He wanted to shout that he could not only walk but run.

'Get up and get these men back to the rubber, and hold 'em there. Any argument, shoot. I'll take the other side; there are two machine guns firing slap down the road, so be careful; keep under cover of the causeway as far as possible.' Holl went up on to the road on all fours, and more or less flung himself across and down into the mud on the other side.

The effort of getting himself back to the rubber sobered Alan, and he was able to start rallying the men, until about five minutes later the Japanese launched a heavy attack on the Australians' perimeter from the west and from the south; with the attack came artillery fire, tearing the trees open like matchwood. The attacks continued all afternoon, and through it with a despairing ferocity Alan sought out his men from all over the Australian position, shepherding them back to an area on the perimeter that the Australian C.O. had allotted to Holl. Eventually they rallied some one hundred and seventy of their men in fairly good order, including five tough and steady V.C.O.s and three officers – Holl, Alan and the other company commander, George Wilkins. Dispersed along a front a quarter of a mile long they had dug in, and they were holding well, but the main attack was elsewhere, and the Australians were running short of ammunition. Holl got more and more grim.

Just as dusk was beginning, Holl was summoned to the Australian battalion H.Q. When he came back he called Alan and George Wilkins. He looked at them for a moment in silence, sucking his teeth. Then he grinned suddenly and wolfishly. 'The Australians are pulling out soon after dusk. They got their wireless going long enough to get an order through from Brigade – there's no hope of any relief from that side, and their orders are to disengage and make their way back to the rear battalion as best as may be; they'll be slipping out by companies, leaving one company as rearguard. That big puff about an hour ago was a direct hit on most of what was left of their ammo, and most of the Motor Transport copped it too; it's suicide to stay here. We've got to make our own getaway, so I'll be taking us out north and then northeast and so round to Brigade.'

He paused.

Alan thought tiredly that it was possible they might escape. An idea struck him. 'Christ! What happens to the wounded?'

'Ah,' said Holl, and sucked. Then he turned to Alan. 'The Australian rearguard is going to force a convoy through down the road, including the wounded. That is, they're going to try, and I wouldn't put it past them to do it. But if they can't, their orders are to abandon the wounded; the padre and the M.O. have volunteered to stay with the wounded. Personally I believe they will get through; they've cleared the road a good way down this afternoon. In fact, they – ' Holl stopped, sucking.

'What?'

'They found the bodies of the C.O. and the adjutant; said it looked as though one mortar shell had got them both.' Holl sucked again, and the other two were silent. Then Holl swore very earnestly for some time, and then said: 'God rest them both.'

For a moment Alan saw the figure of Scrapings in prayer shielded by the embarrassed adjutant, but he had to persuade himself almost aloud that they were dead; it seemed to have little significance. He formed up a scum of swear words in his head, but did not say them. Instead, after a silence he said: 'What about our wounded?'

Their own M.O. had vanished, and their wounded were under the care of the Australian casualty station.

'Well,' said Holl. 'Someone will stay with the Aussie rearguard, with a section to look after our boys.' He sat calmly now, with his legs crossed, his hand resting on his thigh.

Alan said slowly: 'That'll be me.'

'I think that would be best,' said Holl. They all turned involuntarily, as an outburst forward signalled another attack. Then Holl went on: 'If you have to, if you *have* to, you must leave our wounded with the Aussie padre, and get the section out and any walking wounded there may be. But I don't believe you'll have to.' He touched Alan gently on the shoulder, and smiled. Then he turned to George Wilkins. 'And now, George: our move...' Lucidly, he gave his orders.

An hour later it was fully dark. Air activity was over for the day, and so too seemed to be the shelling. The Australian rearguard company was making a great deal of noise well forward, apparently engaging the enemy's attention with success, for two Australian companies had already slipped away through the perimeter on the south into jungle. George Wilkins had just led out his detachment to the north; Holl was about to move with the remainder of the Indian troops.

'Goodbye, Sam,' said Alan to the anonymous figure that turned towards him in the gloom. The Japanese were shelling the north-western perimeter again, and it was noisy.

Holl gripped Alan's arm so that it hurt, and said something

inaudible. Then he tugged at the pack on his back and slipped something long and cool into Alan's hand; it was the Martini bottle.

'You keep it,' he shouted. 'It burns up my guts and gives me wind. Christ, for a pint of bitter! But take a swig for Auld Lang Syne, and good luck, laddy.'

He turned to go, and the ghost of a grin and an exclamation hung in the darkness. Alan winced as the exclamation reached him.

'Abyssinia'll.'

He uncorked the bottle and put it to his lips. It was nauseating, clogging his mouth. He spat, remembering again Communion wine – but it was not like Communion wine, it was the aftertaste of oversweet drinks provided by young ladies in Newnham College, Cambridge. He had just broken from the arms of Lettice; clamped to her, separated only by several layers of winter woollies in that starry cul-de-sac, the closed end of which is the portico of Newnham, they had muttered vows and oaths. Flushed and randy, cleft from her by the stroke of twelve, he was making his way back not without relief to climb in at the time-honoured and classic entry to his college.

An explosion too near for comfort awoke him, and he was alone in a dark and empty wood. No, he was not alone, at his heels tagged Sundar Singh, faithful as his shadow. He swore to himself, and groped his way back through the fearsome trees to the road, half a mile away. The night smelled damp, acrid with cordite and sweet with something that was not blood but the tropic decay of flesh. He licked his lips, and was very cold suddenly.

The shelling had stopped; light arms fire was fairly brisk forward, but when Alan reached the road he found there a tense and silent group waiting round the remaining Australian trucks. With them was one bren gun carrier, and in the trucks were the badly wounded. Forward, almost a mile away, there was only one Australian platoon in position, loosing off, giving a forceful imitation of a whole battalion. The major part of the evacuation had been carried out successfully with efficient speed, apparently without the Japanese having a notion that it was going on. Now the rearguard was ready to go.

It seemed not altogether impossible. There had been no attacks from the rear for at least two hours, and the captain in command of the rearguard had a faint hope that the Japanese might have withdrawn altogether from that area for the night as they seemed to have the night before; there might be a chance that they could rush an M.T. convoy through and save the wounded from being abandoned.

The bren gun carrier that was to make the preliminary probe chirred out of the rubber on to the road; all the trucks in hopeful sympathy started their engines, a series of short whirrs like insects rousing for the night. Straining, the eyes of those in the rubber went after the carrier. It seemed almost over the causeway and into the cutting without provoking any reaction, when abruptly the darkness spurted and streaked flame, orange and red. They saw now clearly the carrier's shape, black against the fire, for only a split second until it seemed to explode in a convulsion of flame.

Fifty yards within the rubber, the watching men congealed. Alan was crouched against the wing of one of the vehicles that was waiting to go; it throbbed gently with the engine against his body. Then, under his hand, the throbbing died. The driver had switched off. It was as though Alan's heart had stopped; he clung, frozen, against the metal, his eyes filled with the glare of the burning carrier.

There was no more firing after a few minutes; the glare died to a glow. The boom of Alan's heart roused him again to fear and to movement, and he went stiffly down towards the edge of the rubber. The Australian captain stood there in silence, in the middle of the road, facing the padre, a short figure who was wearing a neatly belted mackintosh and no hat.

The padre was saying in a sad but calm voice that the captain should never have tried. 'They knew it, Frank,' he said to the captain in that low voice with the twang. 'I saw Jimmie's face as he moved off, God rest him. He knew it. You can't make it. So you'd best get weaving now, man, before it's too late, and get your boys out of here. We'll be all right. Go along with you now.'

The captain stood in silence.

'I'll be all right,' said the padre, in his low even voice.

The captain took off his helmet, and took the padre's hand. He began to say something, with difficulty, and then cleared his throat with an astonishing loudness, and said: 'Thumbs up, Johnny boy. See you in Melbourne if not before.'

'Why, yes,' said the padre. He unlatched his hand. 'Now you get out of here. I've got everything I want, and I don't want you. The Japanese will respect the Red Cross, but not if they find you warriors around. You get along; you scare me.'

From watching the captain go, he turned, to find Alan. 'You too,' he said. 'Take such of our dark brothers as can walk and walk 'em out of here.' He peered forward in the dark. 'We haven't been introduced. Name's Mayo. John Mayo.'

'Alan Mart,' said Alan. 'I'm staying. I've my wounded.'

'Alan Mart,' said the padre. 'That's nice. But don't be foolish, Alan; this ain't your job, your job's out there knocking hell out of these heathen bastards. Excuse my language. And if they catch you here I shall get hurt when they arrive. Get along with you now; I'll see your boys are all right. That's my Job.'

He held out his hand; it was warm and dry.

'Bless you,' said the padre. 'Goodbye, Alan. I'm glad to have met you; I'll look forward to our better acquaintance.'

His hands turned Alan about gently and firmly.

'Goodbye now,' said the low twanging voice behind Alan.

Moving, slow in agony and wonder as if in water, Alan found he could do what he had to do. He heard his voice, calm and confident, telling the Indian wounded who was to look after them, and saying farewell. He collected his section of men plus some stragglers, and a few walking wounded. Then as they waited for him, he stood still for a moment. The padre's back was towards him; he stood looking down the road to the feeble glow that had been the carrier. Alan's hands moved helplessly, and in one of them he found, clutched like a club, the Martini bottle. He took two steps to the padre, and said almost roughly: 'This is vermouth; some of your blokes might like it. Mine won't touch it.'

He thrust it into the padre's hands, and turned almost running, staggering.

From the edge of the northern perimeter he set off with his little band on the route Holl had gone before him. The silence after battle now was deep and treacherous, and they went blindly through it down a narrow path through young rubber into jungle. Branches and thorns lashed at Alan's body and snatched at his clothes; his mind was as quiet and lonely as that road in the rubber where the small man in the raincoat stood with his hands in his pocket by five trucks full of maimed men, waiting.

When they came clear of the path, the moon was rising, and they were in the no-man's-land that often lies between virgin forest and human cultivation, a desolation where the edge of jungle has been burned back, covered with low bristly scrub, and peopled by the rare sparse skeletons of giant trees, fired to death but still standing, leprous with moonlight, and silent, and desert.

They moved east into the brilliant staring face of the moon. Its shine was unnerving and hostile, exposing them as they crawled minute and vulnerable as ants over that burnt-out floor. The silence drained from Alan's mind, and he heard the careful scuffle of their progress loud enough to waken the dead. He hissed, swearing at his men for less noise. They went on; soon sweat was pouring from his body, and his left hand, with no weight like his right hand with its revolver to calm it, roved groping in front of him. It was nearly an hour since he had left the padre, but it was not until they had gone a little way under the moon that the little group of men stopped simultaneously, turned southwards, motionless.

The throb and racket of the final Japanese attack had begun a mile or so away. Arcs of fire, red, yellow, orange, streamed across the sky; flares splashed glaring whiter and brighter than the moon, and sank slow as thistledown. The display raged in brilliant and beautiful violence, seeming to come from fore and aft of the position they had just abandoned, for perhaps twenty minutes, half an hour – then, over the deep clamour of explosives, there came the howl, thinned by distance but piercing eardrums like a glacier wind, of the Japanese infantry going in for the kill.

Alan's eyes closed, and he rocked where he stood. The triumphant maddened howl was edged now by a scream that reached into the bowels of the little group who stood there listening, dragging every nerve in their bodies out searing through the skin. When Alan's eyes opened again, the tears were flowing down his face, blurring the southern sky that now was lit by the pulsing leaping flame from trucks on fire.

Turning away into the swimming moon, he started to move again, reaching for each breath with a gasping jerk of his head. His dazed men stumbled behind him. The desolate earth lurched about him. Across the moon, jerking like a doll in the back window of a car, hung the stiff figure of a little man, his hands in the pocket of his mackintosh, his feet apart. Towards this figure Alan went, on and on, as if in prayer for strength and skill to kill them all. He groped interminably through the gutted world towards the dangling figure, loading it like a crucifix with love and hate. Somewhere he would find Holl; with Holl he would kill them all. Gradually the moon steadied; the little figure stood still and quiet in Alan's mind, and it had Holl's face.

Some time later – they had lost the rough path they had started on, for it had swung away to the south – Alan realised his party was too exhausted to continue without rest; their progress had slowed almost unbearably, a slow clambering over fallen trunks and an endless struggle against resistant bush. They settled uneasily, as best they could, with two sentries. It was 2a.m.; Alan thought they would sleep for three hours, and he was to share the last half-hour's watch. His spent body, undeterred by the ceaseless assault of ants and mosquitoes, passed, almost immediately he touched the ground, into a senseless coma, but his mind ached on, drenched by a flooding moon, apprehensive as an empty stage awaiting action. When he was roused, the world was no more than an extension of his dream; twenty yards away from him, Sundar Singh, who was sharing the watch with him, occasionally moved slightly, but between the two of them their companions lay shrouded in shadow like the dead, and endlessly about them under the moon stretched the silver-grey desert with its extinct totem trees. To the south and west the rumble of gunfire was like distant surf, and once a flight of invisible bombers thudded through the sky. In this ghostly world he found himself a stranger to all that he had ever been, infinitely small in the hostile desert whose every shadow held a threat, but now at last committed in himself to war, in purpose as ruthless and cruelly single-minded as an animal in search of food. All by which he had valued life was scoured from his mind, and, it seemed, almost from memory, stripped away and discarded as luxury; his comforts, his hopes, his loves lay dead under the night's pale shine, grey as ashes, burned out by the white-hot cry of massacre; there was nothing that could not be abandoned and burned.

Until this day he had been play-acting, with the consciousness never quite lost that this appallingly absurd battle was but an ephemeral action into which one had been tricked but in which, according to the conventions of men, one had to put on as good a show as possible, however badly cast. But there would be intervals, drinks at the bar and a critical discussion in the light of reality with tried friends; at the end one went home to supper and to the comfortable bed: home. But there were no intervals, no final curtain, and Hamlet's question was not: to be or not to be – but: to kill or be killed. George had been right in a way; personal survival before death was the order of life, but just survival pure and crude would be more accurate. This was the motive that made the world go round; its urgency, once revealed in action, left no time for personal regrets – it was indeed impersonal. Those who died were but food for the necessary survival of others; life fed on death.

Alan breathed deeply in the freshening air before dawn; he sucked in great lungfuls, and with it the taste of his own unwashed, acrid and sweaty body. A great fog seemed to have passed. His bullet scratch, over which an Australian orderly had stretched a contemptuous piece of sticking plaster, began to itch; his skin was shivering. He felt nervous, and strangely powerful. It was time they started. His belly rumbled, and he thought that they must find food soon. He belched like a trumpet, and roused his men.

'Hold fast, Sammy,' he said to the world at large. 'We're on our way.' As if in answer, the air to the east began to thud with battle.

He reckoned at this point that a sweep round to the south would bring him to the brigade perimeter (if it still existed) in a matter of an hour or an hour and a half; it was not more than four miles. He had not reckoned on jungle, into which his compass took him after half an hour's march. This was true virgin jungle-swamp, with a maximum visibility of twenty-five yards; gigantic trees thrust their way up to an invisible sky, and about their roots a dense armoured undergrowth fought for living space. Almost every yard had to be cut, and every twenty-minutes a halt to be called that they might burn off the leeches that clustered on their legs, unwieldily corpulent with their blood yet tenacious, yielding only to the red-hot end of cigarettes. One of the walking wounded had now more or less to be carried; his mind was wandering and they forced their way on to a continuous delirious babbling in some Punjabi dialect.

At times Alan thought, sick with frustration, that they must be going in circles, but the noise of battle was growing louder all the time, and after more than five hours' despairing hewing and hacking, they at last hit a track that seemed to be going in the right direction. But they moved faster now, and in spite of another stretch of pure jungle, about two o'clock they contacted Indian troops – a jumpy section concealed at a fork in the path. Ten minutes later Alan was shaking George Wilkins warmly by the hand. George looked strangely spruce and obviously just shaved, but his bright blue eyes were too wide and strained.

'Welcome home,' he said. 'The more the merrier, for the jam session. God, we're in a spot; as nice a little spot as you'd never dream of.'

Holl's breakout had been unmolested, and he had made a much faster forced march, with hardly a halt, than had Alan, going more to the south and reaching the brigade perimeter at dawn and at a crucial moment. A few minutes earlier dive bombers had attacked Brigade Headquarters in strength and with devastating and obviously well-informed accuracy. Most of the transport had been annihilated, and two direct hits had been scored on the bungalow where the brigadier was holding conference.

George passed a hand a little shakily across his forehead. 'And may I never see a shambles of that order again! The brigadier was the only officer who came out recognisable and on his legs and he was pretty dotty. The whole H.Q. would have been wiped out if we hadn't arrived in the back of the Jap infantry attack just as it was going in. Maybe the brig. had no idea the Japs were there but the Japs certainly didn't have any that we were. Christ, what a shambles! Nobody knew where they were going or who anybody was. But Sam took us in like Panzers and we just hit everything yellow until we found ourselves hitting Sappers and Miners instead of Nips. So we turned us around and fought the other way. Went on for about three hours. The brig. was killed leading a counter-attack personally, and Sam seemed to go crazy and went out with a section to bring his body in. Got it too. That left Sam in command of all our remnants and the remnants of Brigade H.Q. and all assorted bottle-washers. Sam held the bleeding perimeter more or less with about four men while I staged a rather pretty withdrawal here. Got everything out, wounded, the cooks, even a couple of trucks and, glory, one of those death-traps known as bren carriers. And here we all are and what happens next even God doesn't know.'

'Here' was the fringe of the jungle; a deep bay had been burned into it, where a rough track ran in from the rubber beyond. Most of Holl's troops were grouped actually in the jungle, with strong outposts on the edge commanding the track and burned out no-man's-land between jungle and the beginning of the rubber. Behind him and on each flank Holl had jungle, at least theoretically 'impenetrable', in front of him, the rubber and Japanese.

'They're just building up there,' said George. 'They'd not bothered to allocate many troops to do our brigade; imagine they thought it was a push-over, and anyway I guess they're concentrating on the Australians – that's what that bloody great noise is to the south. And anyway they know we're cooped up here nice and tidy, and when they've got time they'll do us.'

'We'll have to skip through jungle.'

'We've got upwards of seventy stretcher cases.'

Alan stared at him coldly. Then he said: 'Where's Sam?'

'Asleep.'

'*Asleep*?'

'I made him,' said George. 'He was acting pretty queer – he hasn't had hardly any sleep for three days. I got an hour myself, and a shave, and then I spoke to him.' He grinned wearily. 'Makes all the difference. You'll find him in the coffin factory, a couple of hundred yards down that track.'

'Coffin factory?'

'That's right. Handy, as you might say.'

The coffin factory proved to be an area cleared of undergrowth, though shadowed by great trees; it was bounded on one side by a stream, a small river almost, some fifteen feet wide, running fast with troubled, muddy, yellowish water. Felled trunks were stacked here and there, and at the water's edge was a row of vast cumbrous Chinese coffins in various stages of completion. A few sepoys squatted on the ground, most of them asleep. There was a pile of ammunition boxes, and in one of the coffins lay Sam Holl, with his unwound turban draped across him to protect his face from mosquitoes. In the coffin he looked very dead, except for the khaki cloth over his mouth which rose and fell evenly with his breathing. Alan looked down on him, numbed by a sudden quietness. Holl lay awkwardly with both hands resting on his left hip as if on a sword hilt, his crossed legs covered by folds of his turban cloth. He looked like a thirteenth-century crusader, militant, potent still in the sleep of death. But not dead; and in Alan's body there surged a sober but fierce acknowledgment. He stood looking for a little while, almost feeding on Holl's presence; then he sat quietly down at the foot of the coffin to wait; almost at once he was himself asleep.

He roused, startled, he knew not how long after. Three sepoys had brought in a Chinese civilian whom a patrol had picked up in the jungle. Cringing, shaking, with a bayonet pricking his back, the wretched creature whined sing-song. Above Alan, in slow eruption, Holl resurrected from his coffin. Hung with swaths of khaki cotton, he towered bareheaded over the little group.

'*Kya hai*?' His roving eye caught Alan's for a moment, flickered, and rolled on. 'Jennings!'

A portly bundle rolled over some yards away, and sat up blearily. Alan recognised, with some difficulty, the ex-planter who had helped him at his interrogation post when searching for fifth-columnists. The man seemed to have shrunk; his stubbled face hung in folds about his chin.

'Jennings, take this oaf and find what he's got, if anything. If you have any doubts, any doubts at all, shoot him.'

Jennings saluted in a dazed and amateurish fashion.

'No,' said Holl. 'No shooting. I don't want any noise. Just dispose.'

He turned to Alan, and a grin suddenly ravished his majestic and rock-like face. He vaulted from the coffin and took both Alan's hands. 'How d'you get here? Christ, it's grand to see you. You got that convoy through?'

'No.' Alan told him, briefly, what had happened. As he was speaking, Holl passed a hand across his brow, and sat down on the edge of the coffin. The grin vanished, and his mouth started to work as if he were chewing gum.

'So you left them?' he said, when Alan had done. He seemed dazed, his eyes narrowing, searching Alan's unblinking. 'You *left* 'em?' He seemed almost incredulous.

Alan stiffened. A chill struck at his stomach but he drew himself up with pride. 'I left them. I brought twelve men out. Alive. Here, to fight. Those were my orders. I had no alternative.'

Holl blinked. Then he looked away from Alan and rocked a little, his arms clutching his sides. '*Christ*!' he said. 'You *left* 'em. You did.' He rocked in silence. Then he said in a low voice: 'You ran. You ran like you ran yesterday morning. You...' A cold flat volley of filth poured from his mouth as his head turned slowly back towards Alan. His head was thrust forward, his eyes glaring, his lips curling with a muscular voluptuousness as he spoke. His language burst almost palpable on Alan's face, so that Alan had to gasp for breath, shaking, and then snarling like a dog under a whip. He cried aloud that Holl was mad, and then was silent, for Holl's hand held him by the shoulder, holding him up almost off the ground as if on an iron hook; his fingers seemed to pierce through Alan's flesh and meet in the middle.

'You left 'em to be bayoneted in cold blood,' he said. 'Well, understand one thing. I'm not leaving this lot, I'm not even leaving you. I've got seventy wounded men over there with one medical orderly; they're dying at about six an hour. I'm not leaving *them*. I'm taking 'em out with me. *Got that*? I've got about three hundred and forty men, my *jawans*, my lovelies, and signallers, Brigade trash,

Bombay sweepers, the lot. And they're all going out of here fighting.'

His face was about two inches from Alan's, and Alan could hear the teeth grinding as he mashed out his words. But he stiffened under Holl's hand, and said, panting with despair: 'You *can't*. With a soft core of ambulances, it's madness. It's suicide.'

He wrenched from Holl's grasp, and, in a blaze of horror, cried: 'It's *murder*! You'll kill the whole lot...'

Holl's lips drew back from his teeth; the gold gleamed.

'Shut up. I've got a carrier. I've got two mobile trucks that'll tow two more. I'm going out at dusk tonight down that bloody road. I don't leave those poor sods. And I'm giving the orders round here, you pup subaltern.'

'You've got to leave the wounded!'

Holl's teeth showed back to the bare gums. He hissed like a snake, sucked back for breath. 'Mutiny?' he said softly. His right hand swung back, but in that second Jennings came up at a run, excited and voluble, with the news that, according to the Chinaman, there were British troops only five miles to the east. 'Down that path' – he pointed to a track that ran out of the clearing along the river.

Holl's arm sank. He pivoted slowly on his heels, and looked down the path. 'Balls! I had a patrol down there. It runs slap into the river with no path on the other side.'

'But the Chink swears there are boats hidden there, and a concealed track on the other side. And he says there's not a Nip in sight there yet.'

Holl swore. 'How d'you know he's not lying? How d'you know he's not a Jap?'

Jennings was babbling that he was sure the man was genuine; they could get the wounded into the boats.

Holl turned to stare at the Chinaman. Baffled, he waved his revolver at him, and the man screamed.

'There's been 25-pounders firing over there all day,' said Jennings. 'Our guns. There must be British troops. Listen now – there! and there! That's 25-pounders in action or I'm a Dutchman.'

Holl swung in an agony of indecision. His gaze stopped at Alan. He stared at him for a clear minute, his eyes blank, his jaw muscles moving. Then he snapped his mouth, and barked at Alan: 'You'll take Jennings and the Chink, and two men and bat as fast as hell down that track. Cross the river, but *only* if the boats are practicable for wounded, stretcher cases. Contact the British, if any, but *only* if the route is practicable for the whole of this force. I mean, the *whole* of this force: every living sod. That gives you about four hours. If you're not back by dusk – my attack starts at dusk – I shall have to leave you.' He stressed very slightly the last word. The contempt in it was so brutal that the blood rushed to Alan's head; he could not say anything, holding down a murderous impulse to assault Holl, screaming, battering.

At last he managed to say, flatly: 'Yes, sir.'

Holl looked at him. 'You don't salute your superior officers without headgear.' He turned away.

For a few moments after this Alan had talked wildly to Jennings, without any knowledge at all of what he was saying. Then his brain steadied. He apologised to the astounded-looking planter, and set about his brief preparations. He chose his own havildar, who had come through with Holl, and a sturdy sepoy, but at the last moment Sundar Singh, realising he was not to be taken, implored to go so insistently that Alan dismissed the sepoy and took his orderly.

They went very fast down the track for rather more than a mile; it swung fast away from the river, but was broad and firm. Then it swung north again and suddenly they found the river at their feet; on the far bank were reeds and beyond them the jungle dense as a wall. Alan turned snarling on the Chinaman, but the little man was already thrusting through the concealed entrance of a narrow path that ran back down the bank. Alan followed, with his tommy-gun covering the guide. Then he gaped. Dragged up, resting in thick reed, were ten boats of various sizes – enough, and big enough, to get all the wounded over in a swift series of crossings – if the track continued on the other side. The Chinaman was pushing a boat out, and then manoeuvered it, with the other four in it, skilfully about twenty yards farther downstream, round a bend and into a little opening to the far bank where they found what was almost a landing stage, out of which a broad, noble track led into the jungle.

They went down this at a steady jog-trot; they crossed two cultivated enclaves in the jungle, with palms, bananas, and a few poor-looking huts, but no human being in sight. After about two miles, all good going, the Chinaman stopped suddenly, sniffing. Alan looked at him, and sniffed too, but detected nothing, but his havildar grinned.

'Mosquito cream, sahib!'

They went on, cautiously now, Alan glancing nervously at his watch. They came to the brink of another area of cultivation, and stopped. Suddenly, from his right, he heard a muffled but magical Anglo-Saxon oath. In a burst of joy and triumph, he called out.

There was a startled silence in the thicket whence the voice had come. Then a voice said threateningly: 'Come on! Out of it! Show your colour, or we'll sieve you!'

A moment later an astonished sergeant of an English fenland regiment was apologising to him. He was in charge of a patrol out from their main brigade perimeter. There had been contact that morning in the area with small bodies of Japanese from the north, but no general engagement; their road of withdrawal to the south was certainly open. Hurriedly Alan outlined his own situation, and then, leaving Jennings and the Chinaman with the patrol with instructions to ask for cover for Holl's force that night up to the river if possible, he started on his way back with his havildar and Sundar Singh. He had about an hour and a half in hand, and they went back even faster than they had come, Alan as if powered by a jubilant, almost messianic, urgency. As he hurried between the green walls of jungle, an image formed in his mind of Holl's troops streaming delivered back the same way, and in his body that hard and purposeful confidence that he had found the night before, and that had been almost broken by Holl's contempt, ran strong and sure in his veins again.

They were over the river now, coming out of the concealed lair of the boats, when the havildar stopped, pointing to the ground, to a trampled patch of mud by the river's edge. Exasperated by any delay, Alan waved at him, but the havildar insisted. Quite clear in the mud was the imprint of a rubber soled boot, the big toe separate from the others; the Japanese boot. Alan whispered to the havildar.

The havildar shook his head; he was sure the print had not been there when they crossed the first time. Light-footed, nervous and probing as cats, they went on now with Alan in the lead, his finger on the trigger, the others slightly behind on each flank. He was sharp and murderous with frustration; he had no idea what he might meet, but whether an army or merely a patrol, or nobody, he was prepared to go through it. They trod thus, delicate and dangerous, for perhaps two hundred yards; then the havildar gently touched Alan's arm. Silent and still, they listened. From out of sight round a bend came a murmur of voices. They crept forward, step by step to the bend. Sidling, Alan glimpsed some five squat figures in low conference in the near side of the track six yards away, and at the same moment a burst of fire went off so close that for a split second he was stunned by it. Then his finger squeezed on the trigger, and he was aware at once that his havildar had fallen at his side, that Sundar Singh had shot with his rifle from his hip and that a single figure was falling forwards opposite the main group on the far side of the track. Then his attention steadied on the group he was spraying with fire: two of them were falling, another was folding vertically on his knees. One of the remaining two was working desperately at his rifle bolt, and Alan directed bullets at him and his companion, raking them as with a hose. Then there was a confused pile of bodies on the ground. Only one of the group remained alive; a short man, not in uniform but with white singlet and khaki shorts and bare feet. The others seemed to have been interrogating him, and their bodies had shielded him and saved him; he had seen Alan coming and dropped on his knees. He was still on his knees, in an attitude of prayer, as Sundar Singh's bayonet advanced towards him.

Alan snapped at Sundar to hold him, and turned to his havildar. The havildar was beyond help, shot through the heart, and already some seconds dead. Alan shook his head, and shook it again as some emotion passed him by, and went up to the survivor, who was moaning at Sundar's knees. There was a silence, ominous after the brief sudden explosion of the fight. Alan looked blankly at the man on his knees. Some recognition stirred at the back of his mind, but he had not time to pursue it; he had no idea whether the man was Chinese or Japanese.

He told Sundar to drive him in front of them. They were less than a mile from the coffin factory; they would use him as a shield, and he might also have information of use to Holl. They started off, leaving the dead behind them, but they had gone hardly a step when something stirred. Alan swung back, but, seeing nothing, thought it must have been a last twitch of one of the dead. For a moment he and Sundar peered at the bodies; then Sundar turned to go on. At that moment his face was not more than two feet away from Alan's, and as it turned Alan saw his lips snarl up over his teeth, saw the teeth shine, and saw, astonished, Sundar's hand swing up, knocking him sideways. He had just time to open his mouth to swear in outrage before a gun exploded immediately behind him, and a huge blow on his right shoulder twisted him round. He reeled sideways, and as he fell his head crashed into a tree trunk. Then he was down; circles of red-fringed darkness whirled out from a core of blinding light in his head. Bodies were swarming over him, groaning and sobbing, and pain reached suddenly and agonisingly into his stomach from his shoulder. The weight passed from his body, the dazzle in his brain dimmed, and he saw as through a mist Sundar two feet away from him; he was kneeling on the short man's chest, slowly throttling him, his hands buried in his throat. The enemy had only one hand free, and it was knocking weakly on Sundar's forearm, tapping it with no more force than a twig on a window pane; in the hand was a very small, curiously shaped revolver. Alan saw this happening; he could hear nothing and it was like a silent film. The knocking movement grew feebler and feebler, till the pistol tumbled from the hand on to Alan's chest, though he did not feel it. At last the hand itself fell, while Alan heard as if within his own head a rattling end of breath. The dead hand lay on his elbow now, and on one finger of it he saw a ring with a large jade bezel with a dragon. As he looked at it, his mind began to grow dark. He knew what the ring was, what the stranger had been, but he knew that it was too late and no longer relevant, and the knowledge merely confused him at a moment when he needed his last ounce of purpose. Pain was tearing his consciousness into shreds.

'Sundar,' he whispered. 'Sundar.'

Sundar's face appeared above his own. He looked at it, wondering.

It had changed; it was no longer the face of a boy but the grave severe face of a man. It confused him, and angered him.

'Sundar!' he said.

'*Ji*, sahib.'

Alan knew what he had to say: that Sundar must leave him and go to Holl, to tell him the way was clear for escape. He must go quick. In the middle of the teeming, devouring pain, the words took shape; his mind urged them up to his mouth, but as his mind began to drown he knew that he had not spoken. As he fainted, his mouth said, but in English: 'Leave me.'

He sank, spinning, into darkness. Somewhere outside, lost as a curlew, Sundar's voice cried his name again and again out of a black sky.

SEVEN

SHE WAS STOOPING OVER HIM, murmuring with love, as he lay still half-involved with nightmare. He had been fighting in the darkness of jungle, tearing men's faces open with his hands, sinking back in defeat and rising again on cataclysmic waves of sickness that burst disintegrating in thunderous pain. The pain was still there, but little more than a distant rhythm; he seemed to have withdrawn from it, or at most to lie very light on it as a fakir on his bed of nails. And her green hair moved caressing on his brow as she stooped over him; beyond her green hair was a glint of sky, of a heaven of a pure, cool duck-egg blue and somewhere near amongst her voice the purring ripple of water.

But then he knew that her hair was not green, yet still for a moment managed to hold his waking mind back from the real world. She had not deserted him; she had not written because instead she had at once set out to come to him. She was here, her hand moving over him, mapping his body and plotting his reality.

He could hold his dream no longer. The hand now moved, feverishly scrabbling. A long groan of despair rose from his stomach. His own hand roved hopelessly about, seeking its mate. The pain ran kicking back into his blood, as his left hand found his right hand and clutched it vainly; it was as inert and detached as the hand of a stranger's corpse. The appalling thought that his right arm had been amputated woke him fully. Now he saw Sundar Singh's face, anxious but relieved, brown above through a trailing frond of green leaves that touched Alan's forehead. He found himself propped against a little pile of branches, packs and equipment; he was all in one piece, only he had no sensation in his right hand. Across his right shoulder the shirt had been ripped open; under the armpit and over and across his body were swathes of crude bandage made of Sundar's turban, and the rest of Alan's shirt and the right-hand side of his shorts was stiff and sticky with blood. With great caution he stirred all down his body; he found he could move. Looking down at the watch on his wrist, he saw, with a faint shock, that it too was still going. He realised that the hands pointed to six o'clock. As he grasped that this meant six o'clock in the morning, the urgency of his interrupted mission rushed his body; it sat up with a jerk and he almost fainted for pain. But he steadied, balancing, still sitting up. Sundar was fussing about him with little whispering exclamations of fearful excitement, but Alan could not for the moment move farther, and looked at him bleakly, without hope.

'You should have gone,' he said. 'You should have gone.'

Sundar's cheeks drooped with bewildered dismay, and then clenched with anger. Of course he had not gone. There had been a great battle in the night, over there – he pointed in the direction of Holl's position, downstream – so he had half-dragged, half-carried the sahib into hiding in the jungle at the river's edge, had washed his wound, and dressed it. Such a lot of blood, such a lot of bandages needed, his poor turban – for a moment Sundar was hysterically almost merry – but only a very small hole through the shoulder. Sundar held up his thumb and forefinger very close together, indicating the size of the hole. Nothing broken. So they had stayed all night. The sahib had been very sick. But now, if the sahib could move, it was only a very short way to the boats; they could slip across and make their way back to the English troops.

Alan gazed at him stonily. Without the turban, the round face had lost the adult composure that he had seen in it the night before; it looked boyish and stupid. He tried to find out whether Sundar had any idea what had happened during the night, but Sundar had none, apart from the certainty that there had been a great battle with great noise. For all Alan knew, Holl might still be there; there was no sound of action anywhere near, only the rumble far away to the south. His thought stopped at Holl as a terminus. There he had to go.

With careful deliberation he got to his feet on Sundar's arm. He found that, with a crude sling made from the last remnants of Sundar's turban for his right arm, he could move. The pain seemed to be mainly in the head, and from the giddy assaults of nausea in his stomach as he stood, swaying, he thought that he probably had some kind of concussion. But he could walk, though the ground rose through each step, jarring on the roof of his brain. He could not put on his webbing, so Sundar arrayed himself in two sets, his rifle slung over them across his back, the tommy-gun at the ready in his hands. Alan's revolver had disappeared; it seemed of little importance as he knew he was a hopeless shot left-handed. But Sundar had a few hand grenades, and one of these Alan put in the left-hand pocket of his shorts.

So equipped, he climbed painfully, slowly, back towards the track.

'Now,' said Alan. 'You go to the boats, cross the river, and report to the English troops. They will take care of you. I go the other way.'

At first Sundar did not understand. When he did, his eyes filled with tears. He stood for a little staring at Alan, then half-turned as if to obey, only to swing back fiercely. His mouth was trembling.

'No. Where the sahib goes, I have to go too.'

'It is an order.'

Sundar dropped his eyes, but stood firm. Alan felt his temper slipping; he swore savagely at Sundar, willing him away with all his strength until his head started to swim and he nearly fell. He staggered, and Sundar caught him with one hand. He looked into Sundar's face with weak hatred, but could not speak. When he was able, he turned away, spurning Sundar, and started to walk. At a distance of about five yards, Sundar followed; when Alan looked around, he stopped, but followed on directly Alan started again.

They moved thus for some way until they reached a fork in the path that Alan could not remember; he stopped, trying to work out which was the right way back to the coffin factory. Sundar came close up behind him and stopped in his turn, and at that moment they both heard the patter of men moving fairly fast on soft earth. Sundar caught Alan's good arm, and almost lifted him some ten yards down the left-hand path and into the shelter of a great trunk that had fallen along its edge. Crouching behind this, they heard the swift steps come up to the fork on the other path, and there stop. They heard voices, a swift muttered interchange, not Indian nor British, nor Malay. After a sickening pause the running footsteps of the Japanese started off again, down the track towards the boats.

Alan's face was running with a cold sweat. He looked at Sundar, too shocked to be able to make any decision, and Sundar's face twitched with something that was almost a smile and he jerked a thumb down the fork that they were already on. There was no other reasonable choice. They went on, together now.

They walked carefully, painfully, in agonising slowness, for about two hours. The track appeared to be swinging them round south and west through the jungle, though it was difficult to be certain of any direction; the path wound like a dark green tunnel and the sun was hardly ever visible. As Alan settled to a motion, almost crabwise, that was easiest for his bruised body, a faint hope began to revive in his mind. They should, he thought, come out somewhere south and west of the position Holl had been in, perhaps even into Holl's progress. But when at last they reached the jungle's edge it might have been anywhere: the same burned-out wasteland, and beyond that the high ordered ranks of rubber trees. There was no sign of life.

They crossed over into the rubber, Sundar almost doubled up over his tommy-gun, and went up a long rise through the rubber that seemed to Alan's tiring legs endless. But they went up it fast, driven by the relative openness of the rubber wood and by some urgency, a breath of instinctive hope driving them like a freshening wind in a boat's sails; Alan's head thudded as if it must crack open at each beat of his heart. Then they came to the crest of the rise, and both stopped so suddenly that their attendant swarm of mosquitoes brushed for a second against the backs of their knees. Sundar gasped, and flung out a trembling hand, pointing.

Forward from their feet the ground went down sharply, and at the bottom not more than a hundred and fifty yards away was a road, a tidy, metalled road. They looked down through an aisle of the rubber trees on to the road, and across the road, in a little sunlit clearing, were squatting, motionless and silent, some forty Indian troops of their own battalion.

Alan's head reeled. At his side Sundar was whispering excitedly that they were saved, it had all come right. 'There is Havildar Ali Khan. There is Naik Narayan Singh, my cousin, Narayan Singh.' His face rippled and shone, and he turned to Alan with a wild loose gesture of uncontrollable happiness; then, before Alan had begun to realise what was happening, Sundar had set off down the slope at a run, bounding and leaping, waving his tommy-gun, his twin sets of webbing flapping grotesquely about his hurtling body.

With his mouth open, Alan watched. He knew something was dreadfully wrong, but could not make out what. Then he saw, beyond Sundar, the Indians squatting there turn their heads to Sundar's approach; they had seen him, but apart from turning their heads they made no move, no sound, and suddenly he realised that they had no firearms. They were prisoners waiting under guard.

Alan froze. His heart missed a beat; his legs jack-knifed at the knees and he sat with a jolt. His mouth shut, but he could not swallow; it opened to scream and no sound came. Sundar had emerged from the rubber into sunlight, and on the edge of the road he stopped dead. He looked bewildered, his head moving stupidly from side to side. Then slowly, slowly, he started to bring up his tommy-gun, as if it were of tremendous weight, and as he did so, from each flank of the squatting Indians, two short khaki-clad figures stepped out of the shadow of the trees, and two long bursts of automatic fire tore open the silence.

Sundar Singh jerked; his gun skipped in his hands and clattered on the road. His knees splayed open and he sank down. A new burst hit him in the stomach, and he folded sharply forward; the little black pigtail at the back of his shaven head flicked up and down. Then he was a twitching jumble on the road.

A wail, a keening, moaning sob, shook the Indian prisoners beyond. But the bullets that had annihilated Sundar Singh seemed each one to have hammered into Alan's heart, striking in jagged lightning succession till it rent as a tree splits in the storm, and he fell back, unconscious.

When he came to again, he was on his feet, and moving, in a wavering course from one tree to another. He could not have been going long, for the road was still below him, and the clearing where the Indians had sat was still visible though from a different angle. But the Indians were no longer there; there was no sign of Sundar. No one was there.

Dazed, not knowing what he was doing, he made his way down towards the road; he moved in a hallucination – he was not really there, it was his ghost visiting. His body had no connection with his light mind, which accompanied it as at a distance above, watching. There were no Indians; perhaps there never had been – but then he saw a wet smear on the road surface, and a moment later his foot stumbled on something soft in the ditch by the roadside. He found that one of his feet was resting on Sundar's body. He stood there stupidly in the sunlight in the attitude of a big game hunter awaiting the arrival of the photographer. After a little, tears ran down his face, and watching, he noted this, until presently he switched them off. Clumsily, he made his way back up into the rubber.

He wandered thus for some time, as in a maze. Sometimes he would knock his head with violence against a tree, but it meant nothing. His course meandered vaguely parallel with the road, and once he stopped as a considerable number of Japanese troops, squat, sturdy men, joking and laughing, moving in irregular formation, some on foot and some with bicycles, went down the road. It was a very spruce little stretch of road, edged with short vivid green grass, and it was as though he were in England, and these happy people with green leaves stuck in their helmets, their laughing and their bicycles, were villagers *en fête*. But their faces were not English, nor their hurrying shuffling walk. For a second his mind stood still and open; across it went the pattering rush of rubber-shod feet, hurrying and urgent as shellfire overhead, and through it an empire fell like a cliff into the sea, but too far away to hear.

He was clutching a tree as they went past below, murmuring to himself that they were all over the place. He watched them go, and when they had gone, and the road was empty as Sunday again, he shook his head, puzzled, and went on his own wavering route.

After a while he began to walk straighter, with some determination. He had remembered again; his job was to find Holl. He walked on and on through the trees to find Holl.

It must have been about four o'clock in the afternoon that he found him. He had lost sight of the road for a little and swinging back towards where he thought it ought to be, he found himself suddenly almost on it, fifteen yards away from a roadblock. He was looking up at it almost from under it; it was made mainly of charred tree trunks, and it had been partially cleared, enough to allow a single line of motor vehicles through. But riding high up on the heap of trees, as though cresting a breaker, was a burned-out bren carrier. He could not see how many men had been in it, but one man was still visible. He sat upright, brittle as a charred stubble-stalk, the flesh shrivelled black on the sharp cage of his ribs, his head thrust up and back, the mask withered from it in a snarl where shone a gleam of gold; on top, the flaxen hair, untouched by fire, still flared bright as harvest. Its right arm was flung up, as if scorched across the sky, in that imperious order onwards that Alan had seen so often.

Alan's paralysed mind accepted this apparition without question. It was certainly Holl. He stared at it, and could not take his eyes away; yet to begin with it was as meaningless as a prehistoric menhir in an empty landscape. But then his hair began to lift on his scalp, and he backed away from it, at first growling, and then, suddenly, snarling and jeering, loading it with the filth that Holl had flung at him the day before. Gradually he quietened, as at last something of the ultimate stillness, the terrible authority of the outflung withered arm, began to impose on his mind, began to impose an extraordinary order. His dispersed faculties came home like rooks at dusk. Settling, he stared at Holl, as the world too settled to its place and he awakened in it. He was aware now of the sunlit space in which the extinct hulk of the carrier hung with its freight, and aware of the dark brooding shadow of the trees that the upraised arm seemed to have struck in triumph to silence. Beyond that, he was aware too, at the rim of the world, of the rumble of battle continuing. He was alive; he breathed a stench of burnt flesh, softened already by the sweetness of corruption, and from his own body, battered and aching, shot with pain, rose too the odour of blood and filth, of sweat and vomit; but his body was alive. His mind turned on, sudden as a lamp; he saw that Holl's arm was pointing east, and that to the east there was still that sharp thudding that Jennings had sworn was the sound of 25-pounders. It might be that he could make that path again, even in his rickety condition; if he were lucky enough not to run into a Japanese patrol, and the British were still there, he might make it in a day's march; the river would be difficult but not impossible if the Japanese had not found the boats. Urged by a sudden vehement desire, his hope projected back through the dark tortuous jungle tracks to the warm, rough sound of English voices, to a vision of ambulances, hospital ships, cool clean white sheets. His vision brightened like a window from a convalescent's bed; the visitors thronged – his parents, his old friends – and Lettice, sun-warm and fragrant and various as a summer English garden, flooded him with her presence so that he gasped for the wonder of it, and his good hand groped for his breast pocket where was the link, her love written in her letters.

But his pocket was empty. The vision flared, and vanished in a crash of pain. She had never answered his proposal. The letters were in his webbing that lay twisted about Sundar Singh's body and drenched with his blood. Alan's hand ran questing now over his body as if it were a stranger's, as it had done that morning when he first woke. His eyes went back to the black and wizened body on the carrier. They had all died; everyone was dead. He himself was an anachronism of no importance, of no value. His own body had failed him as he had failed Sundar Singh and all his men. It had failed him as he had failed Holl, as Holl had failed him. He stood up; he nodded coolly and almost casually to Holl, and wandered off up into the rubber again, with no purpose, veering like a rotten leaf in the wind, brittle and crumbling.

Towards the end of the afternoon he was still going, faster now, almost in panic, in flight from the sweet stench that seemed to have infested his clothes, even the pores of his skin. His slung arm flapped and jerked. He was almost running when he was halted by the sound of voices, and suddenly he became cunning and sly. He was still in rubber, and approaching a little crest in the ground; he worked forward cautiously and found himself soon on the edge of a clearing. About twenty-five yards away was a bungalow; Japanese troops were looting it, gay and fierce and destructive as children. Sounds of smashing from inside the house came across the still air; on the veranda a soldier was playfully ripping open a mattress with his bayonet. They all seemed so busy and carefree breaking the place up that they had clearly not even posted their sentries properly. Only, almost between Alan and the bungalow, not more than ten yards from him, there was one man not engaged in looting. But he was not a sentry; he sat at a rather elegant walnut table, dressed almost smartly in tall shining brown boots, breeches and a uniform jacket with a white open-necked shirt. He was no doubt an officer. His glistening shaven pate, bent forward, was all that Alan could see, for he was writing on the table, where in front of him a naked sword lay brilliant in the slanting sun.

Alan stared blinking at the sword. He had no idea what to do. It was only after a few moments watching the sword and the movement of the officer's hand across the paper that he remembered the grenade in his pocket. Carefully, he eased it out. He looked at it. It seemed oddly old-fashioned, corrugated, dark brown; it was very heavy but surely much too small; it did not look as if it could do any damage at all. It was, however, something to do.

He considered how he would throw it. It would have to be left-handed. A lob. Something in the long shadows reaching over the lush grass, in the clarity of the noises that came from the bungalow, released a memory in him. He was twelve years old, captaining the second cricket eleven at his preparatory school. It was his day of triumph; in the closing over he put himself on to bowl, and with underhand lobs had disposed of the last two wickets for as many runs, and for victory.

The cold metal was at his mouth. With his teeth he released the pin, counted a few seconds and slid forward out of the shelter of the trees. Nobody seemed to take any notice. Then suddenly the officer looked up. Alan noted the mingled expression of alarm, fury and bewilderment in the officer's face, and swung his left arm back to throw.

As his arm jerked, a sudden and numbing pain stabbed from his right shoulder; he staggered. The grenade rolled a few yards along the ground.

Stupidly, Alan looked at it. A scornful voice rang out of his past, the voice of the defeated captain of the opposing team – '*Well, of course, with dolly drops...*' But it was also Holl's voice.

Grunting, groaning, Alan was half-running now towards the grenade, to recover it and throw it again. '*Coward*!' he said amidst sobs. 'Ah, you murderer. Oh no, no, you *fool*!'

The officer was shouting somewhere, but Alan was stooping over the grenade. It lay there in the grass like the sinister dropping of some prehistoric mammal; it seemed to throb in his eyes, and his hand was reaching for it.

The explosion spent itself in the soft arch of his body, and did no further damage.